Midnight Huntress

A Paranormal Romance

Stevie O.

A PARANORMAL ROMANCE

MIDNIGHT
Huntress

ONYX HUNTRESSES BOOK 1

STEVIE O

Contents

Dedication

To my family...
Thank you for the push to keep going!

Trigger Warning

Content Advisory

This book contains themes and content that may be distressing to some readers, including:

-Supernatural violence and bloodshed
-Mentions of past trauma and emotional manipulation
-Intense fight scenes
-Sexual tension and mature situations (18+)

While this story blends romance, action, and myth, your emotional safety matters. Please read with care.

— Stevie O.

Prologue

"The convoy is moving fast down Interstate-10 going west. You have a twenty-minute window to get in and take out the senator," Jamilah rushed out in my earpiece. I shifted into my panther form and sprinted to the edge of the highway. Bright LED headlights cut through the darkness, their glow sharp against my night vision.

"He is in the second car with four armed men. The first car has two men, the last car has three men, and they look locked and loaded." Jamilah updated me so I could move in.

Golden eyes glowed, heartbeat steadied, the hackles on my back raised as I crouched down to get into position. My smooth black coat allowed me to blend in with the woods when needed. Now sitting on the interstate, it helped me stand out against the light gray cement. My large form helped, as well, when nobody expected to see a four-foot, 150-pound panther laying out on the interstate. The silent black convoy of SUVs were moving in faster, and my panther was excited to be out playing tonight.

I could tell when the driver noticed me in the road. The first car swerved right then left, and finally tried to slam on the brakes, but his speed was too fast. The first SUV barreled toward me, swerving wildly before flipping through the air. Metal crunched, glass shattered—a deafening collision into the ground. I didn't flinch.

The second SUV's tires screamed against the asphalt, smoke curled from scorched rubber as it skidded to a halt. My panther crouched low, golden eyes locked into the chaos. It's time.

Smoke billowed into the air as the car lurched forward, its nose dipped under the force of the sudden stop. The acrid scent of burning tires filled the air, stinging my nose as my pulse hammered in time with the fading echoes of the screech. Seeing all of the commotion, the third SUV maneuvered around the wreckage. My panther was stalking towards the vehicles. Jamilah stated there were three armed men in the last truck. As they jumped out with guns drawn, making their way to check on the first SUV, I attacked. Pouncing onto the first guard who looked to be about 6'2, I made quick work of swiping his lights out with my large claw, that cut through the steel of the vehicle. The other two picked up the pace of running to the overturned vehicle and took out their weapons to take cover. Too bad my panther was faster. Now, last, but certainly not least... what I had been waiting for.

"Five more minutes, Nia! Get it done quickly. You are running out of time."

I stealthily jumped on top of the last vehicle and clawed at the roof to get to my prize. Bullets flew from inside trying to take me out. I chuckled at their weak attempts. Jumping down on the front windshield, I heard loud cries from inside. They were all stunned. Cries for assistance could be heard on the radios, but baby, it's too late now. Should have thought about that before you started the child trafficking ring and brought it to Blackwater Bay.

Desperation surged through me. I gripped the car door, metal groaning beneath my fingers before it wrenched free with a deafening crack. Without hesitation, I lunged inside, seizing the nearest man in a crushing grip. I grabbed him, using his trembling body as a shield for the bullets that whizzed by. Regular bullets did nothing but slow me down. and I had shit to do tomorrow. I released a boisterous and powerful roar imbued with primal energy to paralyze the rest of the guards in the car. Yanking out the senator, I dragged his body over the interstate barrier and into the woods. I needed this to be brutal but quick so I could get my beauty sleep in tonight for my long day tomorrow. One powerful swipe to the gut—his intestines spilled forward. A second slash to the throat, and it was over. Irreversible. Fatal.

My feet pounded against the pavement, each stride pulling me further from the carnage. The wind cooled my skin, stripping away the last traces of adrenaline. By the time I reached my hidden stash of clothes, I was just another late-night jog-ger—sweatpants, tee, and no trace of blood.

Time for that bubble bath and a little reality TV. Another assignment completed. Another shift toward balance.

Chapter 1

Nia Grant

"**N**o! No! No! All of this is wrong." I tapped my pen rapidly against my clipboard.

"The tablecloths were supposed to be hunter green with a gold overlay. This is all green on green, and it's not even the right shade of green. Ugh!!"

A whispered scream came out of my mouth as I walked around the highly decorated City Hall, rearranging flowers and straightening tablecloths for tonight's event. This was the party to start the year, and we would do it right, I thought. I was *the* event planner for Blackwater Bay, Florida. Anybody that was anybody sought me out to bring their ideas to life. I was said to be meticulous and predator-like, in local magazines that featured my business accomplishments. One magazine said I was like a predator stalking prey when it came to hunting and securing choices for my clients for my event planning business, Grant Shadow Events.

Walking in my mother's footsteps made me so proud of all of my accomplishments in this field. With a heavy sigh, I jumped on the phone to put out some fires and knew today was going to be a long one.

Blackwater Bay was a small, quiet town in Florida outside of the major city, Miramar Isles. It held all of the small businesses that brought characters like: antique shops, beauty salons, and mom and pop restaurants. This was a place where everyone knew each other. The big city was where all of the celebrities tended to settle because the nightlife was always popping. Influencers kept opportunities for content in that city. Miramar Isles also kept the Onyx Hunt in business. Big city meant big crime, and someone had to keep everything balanced.

That was where my family business came in. My father started the Onyx Hunt and had all of his daughters working there in some capacity. The Onyx Hunt was a covert organization specializing in high-level assassinations. They were always there to kill people that needed killing. I'm the event planner by day, and by night, the lead midnight huntress. My panther and I hunt at night to blend in with the shadows. My sister, Jamilah, is the analyst and dispatcher for all of our assignments. The twins are also a part of the organization in different areas. Keisha is a detective for Blackwater Bay PD and able to feed us insider intel. Whereas, Aaliyah is our librarian and researcher. There was barely a need for them to get in the field, but we had all been trained.

My father wanted to make sure his girls were able to handle business. He always wanted a son, but it didn't work out that way. He made sure to teach us everything he would have shown his sons. My mother was there to balance out those lessons and keep us as girly as she could. She wanted us to all to be her junior. She was the queen, and we were destined to be the princesses, even if it killed us.

I drew in the scent of the red rose and white lily arrangements from the table decor and then exhaled, casting out the last of her frustrations. All of the fires had been extinguished and things were now back on track for a great event. I'm a perfectionist who *needed* things to go right because my family's name was tied to it. I was raised on the phrase, "Look good, speak well, and perform exceptionally."

My mother, Shirley, was hell on wheels when it came to her girls looking good and performing in any lane to the highest standard. I was no slouch with my clear mocha chocolate skin and my slim-thick frame. That's in my human form; my panther was a different story.

This event was the first of the year at City Hall for hundreds of Blackwater Bay residents, so Timothy and Shirley Grant would definitely be in attendance with their chests out about my representation of the great Grant family.

Shirley will also be on her bullshit trying to pair me up with Blackwater's most eligible bachelor, and I am not here for that yet, I thought as I rolled my eyes. I don't think that the humans of Blackwater are ready to accept shifters. Humans tend to reject things they don't understand and are not like them, even though they were secretly surrounded by shifters in Florida. I had no interest in downplaying my strength to soothe these panther men's insecurities. The panther men here were mostly mated or assholes. A few of them I had dated were raised to think panther women should be submissive just because they were women. That a penis crowned them King and treated the women like servants.

My daddy didn't raise no fool. I knew what I was capable of, and anyone I dated would too. We don't dim lights over here to let a man shine brighter. I would visit dating another species before I settled for a panther man not worth my time. With my luck, that wouldn't work either. I might just be destined to be alone.

There were black bear shifters, panther shifters, and black wolves. Known to the public as red wolves, an extinct species, but they lived in the shadows. Panthers were not pack animals like the other species, so we were pretty solitaire. We would completely miss shifter gossip newsletters if they were a thing. Outside of Onyx business I'm only interested in all things reality TV anyway. They gave me a way to unwind and step outside of my perfect life.

When I was outside of my home, I had to be "turned on" with the perfect hair, edges laid, and clothes slayed. In my abode, I was free to be perfectly imperfect in peace, messy buns and no makeup. Eating whatever, whenever. Laughing loud and yelling at the TV for the craziness these women experienced. I lowkey wished I had the boldness to live life out loud like the women on reality TV.

The Beamers, Benz's, and Bentleys were out tonight. The wolves brought the entire pack out. It was something about that alpha that I wasn't so sure about. He seemed slicker than a can of oil, and I didn't trust him, but the pack spent big money at my public events.

Everything was in order, and everyone was in place, but something felt off. Senators, lawyers, and a few other high pro-file people were in attendance. This event was an opportunity for the decision-makers to schmooze and make under the table deals. Major players rarely came to the small town, but when they did, it was for a grand event.

As I made my rounds to ensure no stone was left unturned, I noticed my mom and dad walking into the event. They had been together over thirty years, and from the looks of it, were still in love. My mom and dad kept themselves in shape and looking good, but I expected nothing less from *the* Shirley Grant. Of course, she was stunning in the latest designer fashion. She wore a Cinderella Divine inspired, off-the-shoulder royal blue Da Vinci gown. She completed the look with Platinum Christian Louboutin Stiletto Sandals.

"Hi, darling!" my mom drawled.

"Hey, baby girl," my dad happily sang as he leaned in for a hug.

My mom leaned in for an air kiss and stated, "You did a lovely job with everything tonight, honey. Everything looks great, and the live band was an excellent addition to the ambiance of the room. Have you scoped out any eye candy tonight?"

"And here we go," I rolled my eyes and whispered to my dad. My daddy was a quiet killer. He was always so calm and quiet until he wasn't, and that's when you should be concerned. He was definitely a great girl dad, just letting all the women in his life do what they wanted until it was time to reel us back in to reality.

"No mother, I have been too busy making sure you have the time of your life tonight," I said sarcastically, giggling. There was a nagging feeling in my chest that I just couldn't shake. My panther was on edge about something. Hopefully, whatever it was wouldn't spoil the night's event. I was about to bring it up to dad when mom called over Barbara Carter.

"Hi, Barbara! You remember my daughter, Nia, don't you? She is the one responsible for this beautiful function. She is the best planner in the world. She even surpasses me. Can you believe that?"

Barbara responded with a hug to my mom, "Yes. It's been a while, but I remember her."

She turned to me to speak.

"This is a lovely event. You did a wonderful job. My son has moved back to town from being away a good ten years. You have got to meet him. He could use your services for one of his many business ventures. He is always so busy being an entrepreneur," Barbara said as she looked over her shoulder at my mom with a smirk. These two were always in competition about something.

"Xavier! Xavier! Come meet the Grant's daughter, Nia," she said.

When this beautiful specimen walked up, my heart stopped in my chest, and the beating picked up in my pussy. Where was this man when we were growing up? I don't remember him looking like this when we were younger. Time away had done him well, I see. As I tried to catch my breath, two of my sisters walked up. Aaliyah, the calm peacemaker, and Keisha, the inquisitive harasser, the twins was what we called them, but they weren't real twins—more like Irish twins. I guess that was when mom and dad couldn't keep their hands off each other.

As soon as they saw Xavier, both sets of eyes gave me a knowing look. He was just my type—athletic build, a rich, dark brown skin tone, and a strong jawline; strong enough to hold my weight.

I don't know what had gotten in to me. I hadn't been in his presence in more than ten years. I don't even really know this man, but there was something primal about my want for him—even if just for one night. I could get my itch scratched and send him on his way. I don't do relationships. They brought out feelings. Feelings were messy. Messy was not a good look for Grants.

Straightening my back, I shook my head to refocus my thoughts back to the event. The night was going well. The guests were dressed great, and the music was a vibe. Everyone was in attendance but Jamilah. She must have still been sulking about not being invited to the family panther run. She had to understand, though, it was kind of hard for her to participate in the panther run when she hadn't shifted into her panther yet. If she ran in her human form, she wouldn't be able to keep up and might get hurt, but trying to get her to understand that was like talking to a brick wall. She was as stubborn as the day is long. Jamilah made it a thing every time as if we purposely left her out of family events, like we didn't love her dramatic ass. Maybe she would show up... just fashionably late like always.

Chapter 2

Xavier Carter

A s I turned toward my mom calling my name, I was taken aback by the beautiful sight before me. Holding my hand out for her to take, I re-introduced myself.

"Hey, Nia, I'm Xavier. It's been a while," I said as we locked eyes. Her soft, delicate skin shimmered against the chandelier lights as my massive hand swallowed hers. My heart rate picked up slightly as we shook hands. My head tilted to the side as I took all of her in and wondered what was happening. She was undeniably gorgeous, but it was something deeper there that captivated me.

My mom cleared her throat interrupting our prolonged eye contact. "Did you know that Nia was the one responsible for this lovely event? She planned everything."

"Oh, really! I may need your assistance for a grand opening soon. I just moved back to Blackwater Bay after a long time away, and I need something big that says I'm back and ready to take over the upscale nightlife space. We need to get together and discuss the details," I said, staring intensely into her deep brown eyes.

She smiled politely but kept her eyes roaming around the room. "Of course, I don't mind. Get my number from your mom. I need to go check on a few things in the back really quick. Excuse me for a second," Nia said quickly as she grabbed her dad's hand and rushed away.

She couldn't even hold eye contact with me for long after she spoke. I know she felt the electric energy between us. Or maybe it was just me. I had been single for a few months now and could just miss being around a pretty lady. Nia seemed to be more than just a pretty face. I saw a strong businesswoman all about handling things—the complete opposite of my ex, Alissa. My ex was swayed very easily by what was easy for her at the time. Not a rider for sure. Definitely not one for hard work on something such as a relationship.

As I walked around to network with a few familiar faces, I heard Nia say to her dad, "Tell me you feel that something is off!" as she showed him her goosebumps on her arms.

"My panther is on high alert for some reason. Keep an eye open. I am going to go back over to talk with the Carters as to not raise suspicions," she said.

What? I must be trippin'.

What did that even mean? As I continued to play the background, I watched Nia from across the room and was intrigued when she decided to come back around to join us.

I acquired a skill of reading behavior in the military that had helped me in many different ways, especially business. This skill had saved my life a time or two. With me being a quiet and mild-mannered person, people tended to let their real selves slip through, and I was able to pick up on the slightest change or oddity. When I was stationed in Kuwait, I had a few spies try to get over on my unit. They came in posing as injured civilians. I noticed the children didn't quite look injured but more anxious.

One kid, Khaled, would look to the right at his uncle every time we asked a question. He understood English, so there was no translation needed. His winces were even odd. They seemed delayed as if he had to remember to be injured. I couldn't stay quiet any longer, or we would be playing right into their hands. Sniffing loudly, I asked, "Do you smell that? Something stinks."

Every U.S. soldier within hearing distance was on alert. Weapons were drawn, and we were now all over the "injured family". Turned out, the uncle was planning to lead us to be ambushed at the home where we were to go rescue the others. I always paid attention to the details. The devil was in the details, and I didn't hesitate to act on what I felt. I was quiet, not a bitch. I just tried to avoid getting to the point of having to go in that mode.

Nia seemed...off. Not as prim, proper, and on top of it as she was earlier. She was more mysterious, edgy...dangerous even. I felt it radiating off her like energy from a hot-wired power line. My dad, Jerome, came up with a boisterous greeting to his good friend and battle buddy, Timothy. Every time they got together, it was like two, favorite cousins getting together at the family reunion. Crazy, I remembered a lot of times when they were hanging out, but I didn't remember Nia. Was she there, and I just didn't pay attention to her? She did have a lot of other sisters, so she probably spent her time playing with them when we all got together.

My dad told Timothy he needed to speak with him about some Onyx Hunt business when he got the chance, whatever that meant. It seemed to be a lot I was out of the loop on around here. As much as I would have liked to sit in a corner and watch Ms. Nia, I had an overwhelming desire to be in her presence and engage her in conversation. That was unusual since my breakup with Alissa. She messed my head up so much, I didn't want to be bothered with another woman. Just watching her work the room and tend to the event's happenings moved me.

Nia came and introduced me to two ladies, Keisha and Aaliyah, that walked up. They looked almost like twins. "Nice to meet both of you ladies! I can tell you three are sisters." Nia fixed her hair and swiped off invisible lint she found on both sisters. She seemed to be the oldest sister in charge of taking care of everyone with how she fussed over their looks.

"Yes, we are all sisters. I'm the nice one," the one named Aaliyah responded with her hand out to shake mine.

"We are just missing the troublemaker, Jamilah," Keisha said and laughed as Aaliyah elbowed her and giggled.

That was interesting to know. *I couldn't wait to meet the last one.* Wait. *What am I thinking? Why am I interested in meeting more of Nia's family?*

"Excuse me for a second. I'll be right back," Nia said as she left me with her sisters.

Something was happening, or she felt like something was going to happen. The constant eye contact she kept with her family, told me to stay on high alert for something. What? I don't know yet. What are these people into? As Nia wandered off, I felt a weight lifted from my chest. Her presence had such a gravitational pull to me that it altered my breathing. I needed to get myself together and remember not too long ago, my ex was on some nasty work that changed me to my core. I couldn't go back to that, so I excused myself to chill in a corner.

As Nia ventured off to mingle with the many notable people in the building and work the room, I stood in a corner and watched. And oh, could she work a room. She reminded me of a sexy, fierce animal on the prowl. She moved like a feline in the moonlight—silent and fluid, each step a whisper of power, each sway a melody of untamed grace. She looked up, locking eyes with me brooding in the corner. I couldn't help myself, by the time I realized it, I had pushed off the wall and was walking to quickly erase the distance between us. I grabbed her hand to ask her to dance. Without hesitation, she took my hand then followed me to the dance floor. We settled right in front of my parents dancing as well.

She fit in my arms like she belonged, I thought as we swayed to the sweet sounds of the live band. My mind was enraptured in her softness and caught up in the sweetness of her scent when her body stiffened against me. Frowning, I stepped back when the sound of glass shattering pierced the air. The burning sting of a bullet grazed my skin, as I yanked Nia to the ground. Using my body to cover her, the world around us seemed to pause. Screams erupted throughout the building. My heart raced.

I looked around to assess the scene when I felt Nia squirming to get up. Looking into her eyes, I asked, "Are you OK?"

She seemed unfazed by the turmoil around us as she stared into my eyes. Before I let her up, I needed to know she was OK, mentally and physically. I saw blood on the floor by us. Searching frantically, I ran my hands over her body without thinking.

Nia grabbed my hands to calm my racing mind. "I'm OK. Thats not my blood."

If it wasn't her blood, then where was it coming from? She sat up and reached for my arm. The blood was mine. The pain didn't even register in my mind. I wanted, no *needed* to know she was safe. After what felt like hours without any more shots, I let Nia up from the floor. The entire building had erupted in chaos, and I knew Nia needed to get to work on putting out this fire. People were scared and wanted answers, so I guess our little alone time was over.

Heading over to check on my mom and dad, they were hugged up in a corner. My dad held my mom and rubbed circles on her back. His eyes were bulged, and he was quiet. This was odd. This big, muscular man seemed rattled. A high-ranking officer in the military, that had a few deployments under his belt. My dad's feathers were ruffled. He looked around and found relief when he spotted his best friend, Timothy. What the fuck was really going on? I needed answers.

Before I could get answers about what was happening, I should probably check on Nia again since my parents were safe. Acting suspicious, but safe at least... for now. I didn't see Nia around the ballroom, she must have gone to the back. The wind rushed by me as I picked up my pace to get to the food prep area. As I walked in, I noticed the back door was opened wide. My heart sank. Could Nia have gone outside to see what happened? It was pitch black out there. City Hall backed up to the woods. If the shooter didn't take her out, a wild animal could.

"Shit!" I scoffed as I headed to the open door.

A soft body collided with my chest as I crossed the threshold of the door. Wrapping my arms around her to catch her, I released the anxiety that had crept into my chest. Then heat rose up my spine. My face twisted in a scowl as I thought about where she was coming from. Why would she go outside after an active shooter that clearly targeted her event? Did she not understand how dangerous and irresponsible that was? I stared down into her face with an angered confusion. Before I could open my mouth to scold her about that, she grabbed my hand to rush me out of the food prep room.

"I know what you're thinking." Raising one eyebrow and tilting my head, I stood silent to hear this crazy bull I knew she was about to give me.

"It's not what you think. I just needed to make sure my guests would be OK to leave the ar—"

"By putting yourself on the frontline of danger? That sounds like a good idea," I said sarcastically. We were now back in the ballroom arguing about her safety like an old married couple. I was really tripping and couldn't figure out why I even cared so much. I just re-met her ass less than a few hours ago.

Our parents came over to check on us. They were relentless with the questions, as if we had any more information than they did. Just as I was checking myself, Keisha walked up on us with her phone out asking questions. Nia leaned in and whispered to me that she was a detective for Blackwater.

"Xavier, can you describe what you heard or saw right before you were grazed by the shot?" Keisha went right in with the questions. Now that I knew she was a detective for Blackwater PD, I was more inclined to answer the questions. I thought she was just being nosey at first. She was persistent. Nia jumped in every time though. She didn't even really let me answer anything, then she pulled me away to her dad. Suspicious. As Nia redirected her sister to the other guests outside, the paramedics came in to check on me.

Stepping to the side, they evaluated my arm. Since it was a flesh wound, I was given a band-aid and sent on my way. This wasn't my first rodeo. I just needed them to sign off on me so I could get back to what was going on with the commotion by the front doors of City Hall. Getting closer, the volume of the arguing increased. An older man was standing in Nia's face yelling about the safety of him and his wife. His caramel skin was tinged with red undertones as he continued to berate Nia. She stood there with her head held high as she tried to explain the situation. I noticed defiance in her eyes, her body stiff and her fists clenched. The firecracker was ready to kick his ass, but the businesswoman had to stay professional.

I slid right in between their confrontation and whispered, "Sir, if you don't back your ass up out of this woman's face, yelling. That shot earlier won't be the last shot fired on this property tonight." He stepped back and scoffed. He must have felt the seriousness of this situation as I stood ten toes down in this moment, unmoving. Grabbing his wife's hand, he turned away and walked out of the building. I looked up from the confrontation and locked eyes with Timothy standing in the corner watching. His face held a slight smirk as he nodded his head and walked away.

I needed a strong drink.

STEVIE O.

What. The. Hell. Is. Going. On?

Nia had me acting strange. Shit, everything tonight had been weird, but I had a feeling things were about to get worse. Why was I feeling Nia so tough when we barely knew each other? Was I even ready to explore something with someone so soon? My last catastrophe of a relationship had me real hesitant about trying anything right now. I just needed to find a way to check these feelings for Nia. Now that I was back in town, I would imagine that we might be seeing a lot more of each other. Our dads were friends, and from the looks of things, might be working on something big soon.

Chapter 3

Nia

I needed to stay focused around Mr. Xavier, I see. One of us needed to keep it professional, and it didn't seem that it was going to be him. The way he stared into my eyes—like he was trying to speak to my soul. I was torn between staying near him or finding out what the hell had my panther clawing at my insides to be released. Rolling my shoulders back, I decided to continue to fight through my need to be engulfed in his scent. The vanilla and tobacco notes in his cologne had me weak in the knees and ready to eat him up.

Needing to get away from him, I floated around engaging in conversations with different guests. It would be great to walk away with a few new clients. Maybe see if there were any new prospects in the ballroom tonight, as my mom liked to put it. Since all the shifters that were raised here were real jerks or already married, finding another panther shifter would be rather difficult. These panthers were not my type. How do you demand softness but don't give me a reason to be soft? I think not. I would date a human or be alone before I settled for dimming my light.

One human in particular was at the top of that list. No! He was my dad's friend's son. That's too close. If things went left, it would make life awkward for everybody involved. It was just best if I ignored my feelings to jump his bones. I'd just...take a cold shower when I got home tonight or take my panther for a run.

Every time I looked up, it was into the deepest set of brown eyes I had ever seen. He stood in the corner with a grumpy vibe and watched me most of the night when he wasn't pretending to have a conversation to watch me some more. Finally, he walked over to steal me away from a few guests with a silent request in his eyes. He reached out his big hand, and I slid my palm inside and followed him to the dance floor. We settled in by his parents and swayed to the sweet jazz tones of the live band. The band jammed out to Rocket Love by Stevie Wonder and the vibe couldn't be sweeter.

With arms wrapped around his neck, he held my waist, and we rocked slowly. Lighthearted laughs left my mouth as he pulled me in a little closer. He sniffed my hair and let out a shuttering breath. No words were spoken from our mouths, but his stare spoke volumes. My panther stayed close to the surface. We both enjoyed this intimacy with him. In the middle of the dance floor, it was just us. His smell, his touch, the way he led and took charge...this man was dangerous. As I allowed him to lead us in our dancing, my panther felt a shift in the atmosphere. Something was happening. Pulling back from Xavier, a red laser shined across my eye. Confusion marred his features.

The click of a high-powered rifle drew the attention of my panther. I fought hard not to shift as glass shattered, wood splintered, and screams erupted throughout the ballroom. My panther wanted to take over and protect Xavier at that moment. She was pissed that our intimate time was interrupted, and he was now in danger. Ripping a throat out was heavy on my panther's agenda.

Before we could protect him from the unknown danger we were all in, he was using his body to protect me, shield me. He was lying on top of me cradling my head. He stroked my hair as we waited for more shots to be taken. All his hard, muscular chocolate self was draped over me.

There was blood. Not mine. Had he been shot? Was he the target? I needed to get up and get outside. My panther might be able to still catch whoever it was. Or at least see the person and have Jamilah pull some records to find them.

He looked down into my face to check on me. "Are you OK?" he said, right as he noticed blood laid beside my face.

He frantically roved his hands over my body. Although his mind was checking for an entry point, I laid there and basked in the feel of his strong, calloused hands on my body. A shudder left me before I could contain it. I stopped his hands so I could think.

"I'm OK. That's not my blood." Did he get shot? I sat up and grabbed at his arm. How did he not feel that? I needed to get up and find out what was going on. With any luck, I would be able to head out back and see something. As soon as I hit the back door, I partially shifted to my panther and took off, as much as my heels would allow, to secure the perimeter of the building. I couldn't destroy this dress, but I needed my panther eyes and possibly agility.

Daddy made sure all four of his girls were highly trained in their human and panther forms. Being retired military, he took pride in having us follow in his footsteps and even created an underground business to capitalize on our special training.

The night was eerily quiet as I crept around the building. I dissolved into the darkness of the shadows, as to not be seen. When I rounded the corner moving toward the front of the building, I saw a small figure packing up and jumping in the back seat of a black Yukon with no plates. I decided not to go after the figure but to go back in and attempt damage control if possible. Shifting back quickly, I ran into Xavier's rock-hard chest and stumbled. He wrapped his big arms around me to stable my body, then twisted his face up like someone pissed in his Cheerios.

"I know what you're thinking. It's not what you think. I just needed to make sure my guests would be OK to leave the ar—"

"By putting yourself on the frontline of danger? That sounds like a good idea."

Wait a damn minute. Who did he think he was, scolding me like I was a child? His child. Biting my lips, I folded my arms as he went on about safety. I was not a damsel in distress in need of saving. Normally, that possessiveness would be a complete turn off, but with Xavier, it was different. Although I could probably kick his ass, it was nice to have a man genuinely care about me. Not how he would look if he let something happen to me. So, I kept my mouth shut. For now, anyway.

Keisha approached us on detective duty, but looking over at my dad, I knew I needed to redirect her. We locked eyes, and he gave me a quick head shake as to not engage her. He knew something. I jumped in and answered a few questions for Xavier before I asked her to go tend to the other guests. I needed to get to my dad and find out what was going on.

Jerome and my dad were still huddled in a corner whispering about something. It had to be about what just happened. As we walked toward them, my dad turned to face Xavier and I with a stone face and said, "We have a problem."

He then instructed me to meet them at the Onyx Hunt once I had cleared the place of guests.

Xavier went off to be examined by the medical professionals that finally arrived on the scene. Calming my panicky guests made me clench my temples. I would rather plan ten big events over managing a group of adults' emotions. This was more exhausting than I had the energy, at the moment, to contain. Heading to take a moment to regroup, I was stopped by an angry husband blaming me for putting his precious wife in harm's way.

"Sir, I can assure you that we are doing everything to rectify this situation. Please calm down." As I tried to de-escalate the situation, he stepped closer to me, raising his hands and his voice.

"If this event wasn't open to any piece of trash from the city, then we wouldn't have been targeted. This is your event, and I am holding you responsible for this." My eyes bulged out of my head. Raising my head, I clenched my jaw to keep my composure.

Xavier walked in between the man and me. He threatened to shoot him before the night was over if he didn't stop yelling at me. The man's face fell, and the tension could be felt miles away. He quietly walked away after he looked Xavier up and down. He must have realized he might just get his ass kicked tonight.

Answering questions and getting everyone out of the center went quicker than expected. Blackwater was normally more peaceful than this, but no one stuck around to find out why things had changed tonight. As the last of the catering company loaded up, I headed to my car. The only ones left were the cleaning crew. They would be there much longer than I wanted to be to get all the shattered glass from the carpet. Dragging my body, I set for the door to head to the Onyx. My panther was itching to shift and go for a run to relieve some of this tension.

Going to the Onyx Hunt was the best place to discuss the happenings of the night in private. This warehouse was designed to blend in with the area and be soundproof enough that our victims were never heard. The hidden cameras allowed us to keep a close eye on what's around us so there would be no ambushes.

Walking into the interrogation room, everyone was quiet, and I noticed Barbara and my mom were missing. So, Daddy, Jerome, Xavier, and I sat down to debrief about the events of tonight. Being that I was the only person in the room who was not former military, I felt a little odd as the guys recapped. My dad started with bringing Xavier and I up to speed.

"Xavier, your father tells me that someone is out to get him and possibly the entire family. If not kill you all, at least use you to get to him. The most important question to me is why?"

Xavier sat there blinking rapidly. He watched everyone as he processed this new information.

"When X and I were dancing, I noticed a red light flash across my face, then I heard the glass shatter. It seems tonight, Xavier was at the top of their list." His eyes grew large in shock at the news of what happened tonight.

"Dad, what have you done to garner enemies of this caliber?" Xavier very breathily said, shaking his head.

"That's the problem, I have no idea. I have been out the game for a very long time. Your mom and I are finally starting to enjoy ourselves, and now, this is happening. I don't want her to know about this either. I plan to handle this on my own," Jerome stated firmly.

Daddy jumped up from the table and walked around to me and rubbed my shoulders. I knew he was about to hit me with something heavy. At that moment, my palms began sweating, and I felt a queasy feeling in the pit of my stomach. Was he about to expose us right now?

"Jerome has solicited the services of the Onyx Hunt for this issue. Xavier, I know you have questions, so let me give you a run down on what that entails. I own an underground business that helps keep the balance in the world. Some of the greatest things are born from the toughest times, and we are here to give tough times a little boost. The same can be said for good times. We are the balancers."

My dad stood behind me and looked so proud of his little speech. Meanwhile, I was nervous on how this news was going to be received.

X sat quietly, letting all the new info he just received soak in. I could tell he had questions and hopefully that would help to ease his mind.

"Do you have any questions, X? I am the head huntress for the organization, and it looks as if you and your family are going to be working closely with us until we get this situation handled.

I have all the teachings from my father and years of experience with these type of situations.

"Technically, we have similar training; I just know more about the underworld than you and can look at this situation more objectively. I have faith that we can keep you and your family safe. You all just must be honest with us about *everything.*"

X finally opened his mouth to respond, but nothing came out. I knew he was taken aback that I was tied up in my family business of being a huntress or "balancer" as my dad put it. Being such a quiet, beautiful woman, most men thought I was just good for arm candy.

He finally said, "How will all this work? I don't have any skeletons in the closet or any idea of who would be after my family."

I stood up and looked both men in the eye and bluntly asked, "Do either of you have any women scorned looking for you?"

I waited, holding my breath and prayed Xavier would say no. The look on his face said otherwise. Damn!

Why was I worried about this man's personal life like that? I don't even know him. Yeah, he seemed nice and was fine as hell, but that was all I needed to know about him. I was not in any position to be getting to know a man in that manner. Especially not the son of my father's best friend. That would be all bad if he switched up on me, and I had to kill him.

Chapter 4

Timothy Grant

Back at City Hall

"I love what Nia did for this party," I turned and said to Shirley. We ordered our favorite drinks, mine an Old Fashion, and a Lemon Drop for the Misses. The bar was my resting place to watch the guests pour into the building. All the big names were here, and this gave me a chance to rub elbows with some new potential clients. People always needed killing.

Leaning down to give my wife a stern warning, I said, "Shirley, be on your best behavior. Leave that damn girl alone about finding a man tonight. She is working."

I turned to look at her with an arched eyebrow. She tried to give me her best innocent face with her eyebrows touching her hairline. I knew at that moment, she didn't hear a damn thing I said.

As a simple man, all I needed were my Old Fashions, my family, and my business. Those things made me truly happy inside. The Onyx Hunt was a very lucrative business that took care of my family after my retirement from the greatest branch of the military in the world. Aside from my children, it gave me great purpose to know that I was helping keep the world balanced. No one-sided agenda would dominate any particular sector of the world. We were sought out and contracted by some of the most prestigious businesses, non-profits and even dignitaries. Pushing my chest out at the thought of my success, my wife beamed up at me with admiration, a slight smile on her lips and a twinkle in her eyes.

Needing to have her hands on me for any reason, Shirley reached out to fix my black tie. She moved in closer, voice dropped an octave and whispered in my ear. Her sweet perfume mixed with her warm breath caressing the side of my face, made my Johnson rise.

She said, "You look sexy in this wine-colored suit. I did well going with the Brioni."

Her face glowed in pride at this look. Shirley was serious about her family being dressed to the nines for every occasion. I know I still looked good for my age. My body was still as fit as it was when I was active in the military. The family run on Saturdays helped a little with staying in shape.

This wine-colored Brioni cashmere, wool and mohair Narciso tuxedo jacket turned heads tonight. Women were definitely trying to catch my eye, but Shirley was the *only* woman I wanted. That woman had given me four beautiful girls and stuck by my side through it all. I would definitely "crash out" like the kids say, behind her. Although I prayed for boys, my girls had won my heart. They were the strongest set of women I had ever had the pleasure of knowing. If I could get Nia married, maybe her and her husband could take over the Onyx Hunt, so I could finally enjoy my wife. It was time for "The Balancer" to find some balance before my wife left me. She had been patient through the years with my deployments, work schedule, and secret missions.

Turning to take in more of the room, I spotted Nia walking up. Heat bloomed in my face as I stuck my chest out thinking about my baby's accomplishments tonight.

"Hey, baby girl!" I excitedly exclaimed as I leaned in to hug her.

Shirley leaned in for an air kiss and stated, "You did a lovely job with everything tonight, honey. Just like me. Everything looks great, and the live band is an exceptional addition to the ambiance of the room. Have you scoped out any potential suitors tonight? There is plenty of eye candy available."

"And here we go," Nia leaned over and whispered to me. Nia started looking around as if something was wrong. She told me there was a nagging feeling in her chest that she just couldn't shake. Shirley and I felt the same feeling as well. We chalked it up to feeling Nia's anxiety for tonight's event. We normally took these feelings very seriously, as panther shifters. Following our panther's instinct could be the difference in life or death for us or a loved one.

Shirley called over her frenemy, Barbara Carter. "Hey, Barbara!"

I tuned the rest of their conversation out. Barbara could be so superficial. Women like that made my skin crawl. I understood exactly why Jerome stepped out sometimes. I hated that he got himself tied down to her. All she did was gossip, spend his money, and try to keep up with the Kardashians. That might be why her son moved away and stayed gone so long.

"Xavier! Xavier! Come meet the Grant's daughter, Nia," she said.

Oh, this is going to be good.

Xavier was about Nia's age, and watching these two, I might be able to play matchmaker. He was ex-military; that would be perfect for the Onyx Hunt. From what I remember of him, he was a good kid with his head on straight. His dad told me about his breakup and how his ex-girlfriend tried to lie about a baby that ended up not even being his baby. Dirty! He seemed to have kept his head up even in the midst of that.

I watched as the kids stared at each other in amazement and realized this might be easier than I expected.

Jerome came up loud as always to greet me. My best friend was always a good time. We had been through some good times and some crazy times together. He was like the younger brother

I never wanted. When we first met, I felt like the older brother trying to teach him the ropes. Getting him out of his lady troubles became a weekly event for us. Even when he married Barbara, he didn't slow down.

He pulled me to the side to discuss some issues he had been having. Anonymous threats in the mail and being followed. Said he had to discuss some Onyx Hunt business with me. My back stiffened when he said he thought he was being hunted. My mind went wild, and my panther started to get anxious. This man was my best friend. We had known each other for so long and had been through a lot. I couldn't just sit around and let something happen to him or his family. He had saved my life on a few occasions. At the very least, I owed him my best effort in solving this issue. The Onyx would be happy to help him and his family.

Could this be what Nia was feeling? She pulled me to the side pretty shaken up about something. Maybe it had something to do with Jerome. Something was brewing and about to come to a head, possibly tonight. I noticed Nia and Xavier dancing right behind the Carters. Nia was genuinely enjoying his company. My panther's hackles raised as he paced frantically inside. That's when I saw it. The little red dot flashed across her face. Xavier stepped back in confusion as if he saw it as well.

Time seemed to slow. My chest constricted, my mouth went dry, and heat encompassed my body—my baby girl. I couldn't get any words out. Immediately, her eyebrows drew together, and terror flashed across her face. Her body stiffened as her back became straight as a board. Seconds later, a loud shriek of glass shattering drew my attention in the direction of where the shot entered the building. The glass that covered one full wall was now gone. I covered my wife as we hit the ground and waited for more shots to come. We couldn't shift in that moment with all the humans in the building. We had to blend in with the rest of the room. Anxiety was scented on every shifter in the building. With the struggle of them having to fight their animal to stay inside, the shifters were stressed about staying in control. We needed them to have control more now than ever.

The weapon used had to be a long-range rifle, since my panther eyes couldn't spot anyone for a long way out. As I shielded the love of my life, I looked for my girls and realized I didn't have to worry about Nia. She wasn't shot. From the looks of things, Xavier had it under control. He was also using his massive size to shield my baby girl. When he finally let her up from the floor, I knew she would go after the shooter. So, I checked on my other babies. Aaliyah and Keisha were both far enough away from the action that I could breathe.

Nia was in hunt mode, and I hoped she didn't shift. When she jumped up, I knew she was on a mission to find the shooter. I needed to act quickly to keep Jerome and Xavier inside. As panther shifters, we took pride in keeping our true identity from the outside world. This could blow our cover if anyone ran outside and saw her shift. The only people that were privy to our real identities were our spouses. Even friends, most of the time, were not afforded the privilege of knowing something so sacred. One lost friendship could ruin things for the entire paranormal community. Jerome had no clue about the world he lived amongst. If he did, he didn't hear it from me or my family.

Thoughts pinballed in my head, bouncing from one worry to the next without landing on anything solid.

"Who was the intended target?" I whispered to myself.

Jerome just confessed of a few shady encounters he recently had, but now, I wasn't sure if the shooter was aiming at Jerome or Xavier. My mind was spiraling, and I needed to get to my office to organize my thoughts.

Pacing back and forth, staring at the blank wall in the hallway, I struggled to comprehend how my best friend and possibly his family were being hunted. What could have caused this? Jerome came to me trying to discuss more, but this was a conversation that needed to happen at the Onyx warehouse. Nia and Xavier came to check on everyone. I couldn't wait much longer because this situation was serious. Facing them, I needed to get them alone and soon.

I said, "We have a problem."

I could definitely use this to get Nia and X together. Damn, I sound like Shirley now. We needed to get these people out of here so we could get to my warehouse and discuss this.

A commotion drew my attention to the front of the building where I saw one of the guests arguing with Nia. Emotions were high after what just happened, I get it, but I might have to put somebody in the ground tonight if this continued. Leaning against a column, in clear view of the altercation, I continued to sip another Old Fashion quietly. I was giving him an opportunity to calm down before I decided to put my hands on this motherfucker.

Before I could check this man, Xavier walked up smoothly, leaned in close to his face and lowly said something to the man. They were standing eye to eye. Xavier made sure to use his body to block Nia's view of the conversation. Looking at his body language, you would think Xavier was calm, but the look on his face was anything but. If looks could kill, that man would have looked like he had just left a shredder. Xavier seemed to be protective of my baby girl, and the corners of my lips twitched.

The angry man took his wife's hand and left quickly without any further commotion. This plan was coming together better than anyone could have imagined. Nodding my head at Xavier, I slipped back into the shadows. I needed to drop Shirley off at home and head to Onyx. We had pressing business to handle.

Chapter 5

Shirley Grant

It was going to be a great night. I looked good, my man was looking good, and I was sure all my girls would be unmatched. They already knew the motto, "Look good, speak well, and perform exceptionally," so tonight better be top notch. The Grant name was on the line. The Grant women were known for hosting only the most fabulous events.

If only I could find Nia a suitable benefactor. Tonight had to produce a man worthy of her and this grand lifestyle befitting of a Grant woman.

"Hi, Darling!" Leaning in for an air kiss, I stated, "You did a lovely job with everything tonight, honey." Astounded, I surveyed the room's decorations. "Everything looks great, and the live band was an excellent addition to the ambiance of the room. Have you scoped out any potential suitors tonight? There is plenty of eye candy available."

I moved on to something else, when she rolled her eyes. Unfortunately, I knew exactly what that meant, and she was going to hear about it soon after this event.

My daughters didn't understand the sacrifices I had to make for them to be in the position they were in now. I had worked hard to secure them a wealthy second parent and suffered through all his deployments and secret missions. I had been neglected more than I cared to admit because I needed them to be in a position of power to move about the world in a classy and dangerous manner. My husband raised them to be tough, mentally and physically. I brought the class and sophistication to the table. Well-rounded women received an abundant amount of options in life. They were able to choose what wealthy man they would grace with their presence.

I chose my husband, and even though I had to deal with him being gone a lot, he still cared for me and our girls. We didn't want for a thing, and when he officially retired, I would finally get this man's full attention. I would no longer have to deal with late nights away, long trips in other countries, and dry spells when he was stressed about work. He wouldn't even let me relieve his stress when he had a high-profile client. Sex was the last thing on his mind when he was "locked in".

"Hey, Barbara! You remember my daughter, Nia, don't you? She is the event planner for this beautiful function. She is the best planner in the world. She even surpasses me. Can you believe that?" I spoke.

Barbara went on to introduce her son, Xavier, before I could interject. He was not exactly who I had my eye on for her, but for now, I would let them talk. Shortly, I would be breaking that up though.

"Barbara, let's walk and talk. I see some potential benefactors I think would be great for my Nia. Do you know she put this grand event together on short notice? She pulled everything off flawlessly. The mayor's wife personally told me this was the most elegant event she had been to in a while. Honestly, I don't know how she does it. She works so hard though. We are such proud parents.

"How is Xavier? I heard you say he was back in town. Is he staying this time?"

"Yes, things ended with his old girlfriend. He wanted to come home to be with family. Isn't it wonderful?" She beamed. "My grown son wanted to spend time with little old me. He could've chosen anywhere, and his choice was here with his family."

She said that as a dig to me and my husband's situation. Everyone knew Tim spent a lot of time away from home on different assignments. Some people believed he was with his other family, but I knew my husband better than that. He also knew that I would take everything from him and leave him with just his toothbrush. I had sacrificed too much for him to just walk away.

As she talked on and on about how wonderful her son was, I was stopped in my tracks. My skin prickled, my senses were on high alert—something was happening. My body wanted to shift, but now wasn't the right time. A lady like myself, always stayed in control of her animal.

The fight with my panther was interrupted when my husband came to steal me away from Barbara, I couldn't be happier. Talking to her had bored me, and I didn't want to hear any more about Xavier. I needed to make sure that nothing went further with him and Nia as well. He seemed like a nice young man, but not quite what I had in mind for Nia.

In the rare moment Tim and I were together at a party, we always danced. Dancing with my honey calmed me and my panther. This prickle on the back of my neck just wouldn't go away. Pulling him closer to me, I nuzzled my face in his neck. I inhaled peace, strength, and security from him—the true essence of what I knew Tim to be. I couldn't wait to get home with him tonight. Just then, the shriek of glass shattering caused me to fight my inner panther harder. She wanted to come out and protect my husband and children. Tim shielded me from the chaos in the building.

Tim went to Jerome and Xavier when Nia ran out to scour the woods. I needed to get to my other girls to make sure they were OK as well. I knew Nia went looking for whoever decided that this event was the time and place for their personal vengeance.

At least she was away from Xavier. I huffed to myself. They looked a little too happy to be arm-in-arm swaying to the sweet sounds of the jazz band. Barbara had made her way back to me after that incident since our husbands were huddled up together conversing about something. Her presence had me rolling my eyes before I could catch myself. I could only take so much of her company.

Needing to find any excuse to leave, I said, "I need to get back to my husband to find out what all the commotion was about. You know how he is; he will get to the bottom of this being the former General in the military."

Before I left, I had to make sure she knew that she would never, could never, have one up on me. When Tim and I met, I was in college, and he was in his military career. We met Barbara and Jerome shortly afterward. Since I was the notable socialite, and she was just a simple waitress, she had her nose up toward us, even back then. She would never be on my level, and she knew it. Her husband did too. I made sure I looked stunning, per usual, as I sauntered back up to my husband to inquire about the commotion.

Of course, in true Timothy fashion, he was taking me home so he could go off galivanting in the city to find out who was behind tonight's attack. We almost had a full night of dancing and enjoying each other's time. I understood duty called, especially when lives were on the line. Just another day in the life of being Timothy Grant's wife.

Home alone while he is out saving the world, again.

Chapter 6

Jamilah Grant

"Another successful hit, orchestrated by me," I said, patting myself on the back. "But no one even notices because little Ms. I Can Do No Wrong, Nia, is the lead huntress."

I grunted.

"This organization wouldn't even be as successful if it wasn't for me organizing everything. I don't know why Daddy won't just let me out in the field," I fussed, snatched my things from the table, then slammed them in my bag.

It was definitely time to leave the building after the successful hit on the senator. Walking out of the warehouse, I noticed an envelope on my windshield. Taking a look around the deserted neighborhood, I checked to see if I could catch any movement. I couldn't shift like the rest of my family, yet, but I knew how to move in this industry.

STEVIE O.

Daddy took out all the girls to train on how to fight and be hunters. Being the youngest, I had the most to prove. Nia outshined us most of the time, which put her on Daddy's favorite list. That pissed me off so much because he never noticed how hard I worked or even how much I had improved. For someone who didn't have their panther yet, I thought I did a damn good job. I kept up with three other panthers as a regular human. Who, might I add, had been training longer than I had. He was rigid when it came to our training. Daddy started us at an early age. He wanted boys and let it be known, but *baby, we the best*, I thought in my DJ Khalid voice. This man was always playing in my face when it came to the Onyx Hunt. All this training, and he wouldn't let me out in the field. I was a great handler and hacker, but I wanted to do more—needed to do more. His precious Nia got the top assignments. Rolling my eyes, a lump formed in my throat as I thought through this great injustice being done to me.

I didn't get an invite to the family panther run this morning, as usual. They said it's because I could get hurt in my human form. They always left me out of things, and I was sick of it. I didn't even want to go to the party tonight. It would just be a bunch of shifters pretending to be normal around their human friends. I was supposed to be a panther shifter by now. For the life of me, I didn't have a clue as to what was wrong with me.

Most panthers shifted in puberty, and I was well past that time without so much as a claw showing. Damn, could a bitch get a whisker?! Visiting the spirit guides gave me some hope that it might happen eventually. I was told that sometimes it took a big event or traumatic experience for a panther to show its face and become a protector.

Well, I wish the bitch would come on already. I can't move up in the ranks like this, and she is holding me back.

"Ugh!" Sighing and blowing out a heavy breath, I reached for something on the front of my car. "What the fuck is this on my windshield?"

I snatched the envelope from under my wiper blades and said, "They bet not have scratched the Benz either."

I dropped into the quiet comfort of my luxurious black leather seats. Starting the car, I opened the envelope and a picture dropped in my lap. "Who the..."

Before I could question who the older man on the picture was, I received a notification alert on my cell. It was a text from an unknown number. Holding my breath, I sat staring at my phone, skeptical to open it.

> Onyx may not believe in your skills but we do. Handle this and you have a job with our organization.

Who was this man on the picture? I felt like I had seen him before, but where? I thought long and hard as I drove out of the area and to my home. There, I could do all my research and plan my attack if I chose to take the job.

Sitting down at my desk, I needed to do a little digging on Mr. John Doe before I could give an answer to this mysterious organization.

"Jerome Carter, husband of Barbara Carter and father to Xavier Carter. Former military looks like he served in the same place as my dad. Wait, is this...Oh shit, this is dad's friend."

As the information spewed from my mouth, I almost burned a hole in my carpet pacing back and forth. This was bad—all bad. Did I really want to take the job? I needed to find out what he did first. Maybe if he was out here kicking and burning puppies, that would ease the conflict in my heart.

Ding!

My heart beat out of my chest, and my stomach dropped. It was another notification from the unknown number that I knew better than reply to.

> By now, you should have figured out who the target is to you. Can you handle a job so close to home or will this be a problem?

Palms sweaty, my mind was racing a mile a minute. I didn't know if I could do this to my dad. First, I would be betraying him by taking a job with a rival organization. Then, I would have to get rid of his best friend. Time was ticking. Shaking my head, I whispered into my hands, "I don't know. I don't know. I don't know."

This was a big decision to make, and I needed to give it some serious thought.

Ding!

"Shit. I need to know what he did to trigger a hit on him before I make my decision," I said as I slowly reached for my phone and tapped my foot quickly on the floor.

> Let me help you decide, the target is responsible for coordinating transportation on all of those missing children cases.

Hands shaking, my eyes bulged, and my heart rate increased. He undoubtedly had to die now. "Sorry, Dad, but he gotsta go!"

A few more clicks on my MacBook keyboard, and BAM!

"This is too easy. Home address, weekly itinerary, and every car make and model in his or his wife's name. I'll be seeing you tonight, Mr. Carter."

Decision made. No other questions needed to be asked when children were involved. Sex trafficking had been an ongoing issue in Florida, but we had recently seen an uptick in cases in the last few years.

Finally, getting my chance to shine and prove to my family that I was just as capable as my sisters. I stood before the mirror, tightening the straps on my tactical bodysuit, its dark material hugging my petite frame like a second skin. Mobility was key. I needed to be swift, silent, and deadly. The suit blended seamlessly into the night. Shadows and moonlight my only allies. My long box braids wrapped in a high bun were secured tightly for a more polished look, to avoid distractions and hide identifiers.

My beautiful weapons laid before me on the bed, carefully arranged in the order I might need them. The sweet smell of gun oil, and steel warmed my heart. A compact pistol, silencer attached, fit snugly against the small of my back. The cold metal always managed to ground me when it was flush against my skin. But the true star for tonight—a precision rifle, matte black with an extended barrel, built for distance. I ran a hand along its cold metal surface. A tool of finality. I attached the suppressor, locking it into place with a quiet twist.

With one final glance at my setup, I slung the rifle's case over my shoulder. I rolled my shoulders, exhaling slowly, getting my mind in the zone, as adrenaline ran through my veins.

Getting to the venue early allowed me to scope the scenery and plan for my shot. With a moderate breeze blowing tonight, I had to adjust my scope and shot. My all-black attire allowed me to blend in to the shadows of the hill I found on the side of the building directly in front of the floor-to-ceiling windows. Patience was the name of the game in a situation such as this. The guests came in dressed beautifully, mingling and schmoozing without a care in the world. I spotted my family in the building. Of course, my mom wouldn't miss an opportunity to go to a luxury event. She thrived in those environments. There was my beautiful target talking with dad. Now, Nia and some guy were dancing right in front of him. I didn't have a clear shot. Being such a good shot, I was sure I could take the shot in between steps.

I tracked the rhythm of the guy dancing with Nia. Step, step—one-two, one-two. My finger hovered over the trigger. On two, I took the shot.

"Shit!! I missed." Looking in the scope, I checked to see if I hit the guy dancing with Nia. *She needs a man, I can't kill him*, I thought.

Deciding if I should take another shot, I noticed her run toward the back of the building. I immediately broke down my rifle to get out of here. With all my practice, this was a breeze, and I could do it in under a minute. Another notification came in from the unknown number.

"Damn, DJ Khalid. Another one headass!" I said, looking at the screen.

> Black Tahoe waiting on the side of the building. Go with them. Let's chat!

I didn't know if this was a rescue or a trap, but I didn't have time to hesitate. Nia had already shifted, her golden eyes locked onto me. She couldn't see my face because I hid it with my balaclava just in case. Jogging, I dove into the back of the Tahoe—hoping, praying, I hadn't just sealed my fate. My safety was in the hands of the unknown texter. Hopefully, I got more answers about this organization and its mission. Nia knew she couldn't make too much of a scene with all the guests in a frenzy back in the building. Two huge, masked men sat in the front of the SUV. The cabin was silent as we drove to our destination.

My palms were sweaty, and the area was unfamiliar territory. This was a bad idea. I didn't know these people. I missed my shot. This could be my punishment for not being successful at the hit. The eerie feeling I felt in the pit of my stomach didn't subside until we pulled into the warehouse. I still had my weapons on me, so if things got a little rowdy, I might be able to fight my way out. The calm from a shaky nervous system didn't last, though, when the tall, dark, broody man stepped out of the shadows and met us at the door.

Hesitating, I finally stepped out of the vehicle.

"Welcome, Jamilah! My name is Shadow; I run this operation. I need you on my team."

His voice was so powerful and deep, I felt it in the pit of my stomach. He oozed danger, money, and power. I hoped this wasn't a bad idea.

"Why me though? You don't know anything about me," I said with a surprising sass in my tone.

Why would I talk crazy to the head of this organization when he had all these big scary killers surrounding us? I must be losing my mind.

"I know more than you think I know. I have been watching you and your family for some time now. I have learned some interesting things about the Grant family. I know how bad you want to get active in the field. I also know your pops won't let you loose out there either. That's where I come in at."

Standing tall and looking every bit of the killer, I knew he was, I stood silently and observed everything. This would either be an incredibly good thing or destroy my life.

Chapter 7

Xavier

The light buzz from the AC was the only sound that could be heard in the building. We walked into a building that looked like a regular warehouse for shipping and receiving. The inside was anything but regular. Being inside brought back feelings of the military. Rooms for interrogation, rooms for meetings, and office for intel gathering. The light gray color on the walls in the common areas, was to keep any hostages calm.

The military always played mind games, and certain colors evoked emotions from a person without their knowledge. Gray created a neutral environment where relaxation was desired. Great way to get someone to talk. The Grants were serious about whatever they had going on here. This place looked like a top-notch governmental agency.

My mind raced, who would be hunting my family? Could it be my ex, Alissa? But why would she want to harm me or my family when she was in the wrong? She cheated with my friend, got pregnant, then lied about the paternity. As I went through every scenario of what could be going on, Nia spoke up.

She asked, "Do either of you have any women scorned looking for you?" I knew my face was telling more than my mouth at this moment.

I started shaking my head no before she could even get the question out fully. After I told her what was going through my mind, she had this look I was unsure of, kind of like sympathy. Her eyes narrowed as her eyebrows pulled down in concentration. Worry crept across her face, and then...her shoulders relaxed, almost like she was relieved. Was she expecting something else but pleasantly surprised she was wrong? Was she interested? I knew I was...I thought. How did that even work? She was a huntress—a freaking huntress. She was fierce, but damn, that was unexpected.

Timothy cut into my thoughts. "Jerome and I believe Nia needs to stay close for a couple of weeks in order to gain insight on what's going on that you guys may have missed."

There was a slight smirk on his face.

"I suggest a fake relationship to keep appearances with the public. What do you think, Xavier? You don't have a girlfriend at the moment, right?"

I watched Nia to see how she was reacting to this. She stood tall, unmoving, with her head held high. I couldn't get a good read on her emotions. Timothy must have trained them on more than physical combat.

I must have looked overwhelmed because Nia came over and touched my shoulder, and a spark jolted me back to my senses. I finally spoke, "No, I don't have a girlfriend, and I am down with it if that works for Nia."

Looking into her eyes to see if there was any form of hesitation, I saw none.

"You don't have some crazy man that I would have to hurt if he sees us out together now, do you?" I laughed. She chuckled and shook her head no.

"You can come to my house for a few days. If someone is using you to get to Jerome, they wouldn't think to look at my house. When we leave, you should grab a few things from your house then be my house guest for a few days," she said in a monotone voice, like she was in serious business mode.

"Well, I guess that's settled."

I stood up to announce I was leaving, and Nia said she would drive me. We needed some alone time to figure this new dynamic out.

Leaving the warehouse, I climbed in the front seat of her black and rose gold Cadillac Escalade. This truck was spacious, kind of surprising for a single woman with no kids. "Why do you drive such a large vehicle?"

"This is the business vehicle. I need space to haul all my equipment. I don't just hunt people all day. I do have a day job."

She laughed and started the truck. "I do have something smaller for when I need to look cute and run errands."

Nia drove my dad and I to my home to get some things before we dropped him off. As we were about to enter the highway, I noticed she kept looking in her rearview mirror. Nia sped up and blew through a light, instead of jumping on to the highway. She made a quick left, then made another left. She looked over at me and said, "We have company. Black Tahoe on my right, two cars back."

My dad and I started getting ready. I pulled out my Glock 19, and my dad was right behind me with his Sig 320 from the waistband. We checked the mags. My dad taught me to stay ready, so you didn't have to get ready. All three of us were ready to party.

Nia sped through the city and decided to make a sharp right turn to catch them off guard. "Quick, take a look to see if you can see a face."

Nothing. Her speeds topped at 110 through the city. We were able to lose them without having to exchange any gunfire. We were going to be in for a long ride solving this little mystery. Nia seemed to be the right person to work alongside for this issue. She handled that with no problems.

Exiting the car, Nia walked ahead of me, and I saw that sexy sway in her hips. It was as if she were gliding to the door. I tried not to bask too much in her honey and vanilla perfume. Her tantalizing scent wrapped around me and plagued my senses for the thirty-minute ride here. My dick woke up and was ready to come out and play. That ass was enough to make me forget what we just went through. This woman was taking me too fast and didn't even know it, but I might be down for the ride.

As she walked closer to the door, her body stiffened. I learned from earlier to pay attention to her. It was like she had a sixth sense for danger. She raised her right hand to halt our steps. No explanation was needed as we pulled out our weapons. We immediately got into position like we were back in the military. Normally, I would not be OK with her going in before me, but with this new information, I knew she was just as dangerous as I was. Shit, maybe more. She pushed the front door slightly, and it opened with no hesitation. Everyone was on high alert with guns drawn.

Walking into the hallway, everything seemed to be just as I left it. Being a single man, I didn't need much. I had minimal decorations in the area, just a few pictures on the wall, a small table with a large mirror above it. That mirror gave us a great view of the living area. We saw masked men, one headed toward the back rooms, oblivious to our presence. My dad went after the one toward the back of the home.

When I looked over at Nia, she looked uncomfortable. Her fists balled, jaw clenched, and veins popped out on her forehead. She shook her head like she was clearing her mind of a fog. We both winced as Nia stepped through to the living room, and the floor creaked. The masked man, a few feet in front of me, turned and lunged toward Nia. He threw his body on her, and her knees buckled at his weight. As I ran toward them to assist, the masked man squealed in agony. She had stabbed him with something, but I didn't see a knife.

I threw him to the ground and rearranged his facial features with my shoe. Nia pulled me off the man in an effort to keep him alive for us to gather information later, so I decided one more kick to the head wouldn't hurt, knocking him unconscious. I bent down to grab the guy and saw a dark figure run by the door headed to my office. Nia grabbed her pistol and sent a shot in that direction. My dad was now in the room with us, and she must have felt freer to have a little gunplay with the last suspect left in the house.

Nia breathing hard, stated, "I will call for a pickup for these guys. They need to go to the Onyx to be interrogated. Especially this one." She pointed to the one with the shoe print in his forehead. "Get your things so we can get out of here. We need to keep all of this between just us for now. I need to get a hidden security detail for your mom and dad while we get this worked out."

Heading out of the home, I could tell Nia's mind was running. She looked to be on autopilot. I grabbed her hand leaving out of the front door then whispered in her ear, "Have to make it look real in case someone is watching, right?"

Her eyebrows raised to her hairline. Her hand was soft in mine, and I couldn't help but to like the feel of it—way more than I should.

Dropping my dad off was quick and uneventful, leaving us alone. Finally, we could discuss the events of tonight. Nia nudged my shoulder as she asked, "I know today has been a lot. How are you holding up? What's on your mind?"

My mouth dropped at the fact that she cared enough to ask. I had never been asked that by a woman. This was foreign, and honestly, I didn't have an answer. We sat in silence until I could process everything.

Pulling into Nia's home, I finally had the words. "I'm good. My body is tired, and I need sleep. Just want to figure out what's going on to keep my family safe."

Walking into Nia's home, I couldn't even really take in the beauty around me. She showed me a few things like where the kitchen was, the bathroom, and my room. I couldn't wait to shower and hit the bed. It was now going on three am Sunday morning, and my body was screaming for rest.

Walking from the bathroom to my room, I heard a TV blaring. As I passed Nia's bedroom, she was sitting in the middle of her bed drinking wine and watching a show, with her eyes closed—almost as if it was relaxing to her. It looked to be a reality show or something. Whatever would help her get to sleep after a day that we had.

The sun shined bright as the rays peaked through the blackout curtains that were not fully closed. For a moment, I forgot that I was in Nia's guest bedroom. Crawling out of bed, I headed to handle my hygiene then off to make coffee. Heading down the spiraled stairs, I was finally able to take in the scenery of her house. This place was spacious and meticulously decorated. It looked like something straight from a model home—the complete opposite of where I lived. It wasn't exploding with all the girly frills I saw from most single women. The kitchen was a cook's dream. The latest high-end appliances, a huge island with extra prep space, and an abundance of storage littered this large, open space.

Since I dabbled in the kitchen a little bit, seeing all her top-notch appliances and gadgets, I was intrigued. I decided to make us some breakfast before we got too deep into our day. With a fully stocked refrigerator, the options were endless. I decided to make something quick and easy.

"I see you made yourself at home," Nia said as she side-eyed me. Turning around to see her gorgeous face, I was met with more than I expected. She was dressed in sweats and a big T-shirt. Her hair was wrapped up in a messy bun, and she smelled amazing, not like last night when she was all dolled up. This was something else—something intoxicating. Nia, in her relaxed state, was even prettier than all the glam from the party. I stood there silent, taking her all in with my left eyebrow raised.

"Who taught you this wizardry? What is this, shrimp and grits?" With an elevated voice, she practically yelled, "Are these homemade biscuits? The answer is yes!"

I chuckled. "Girl, what are you talking about?"

"Yes, I will marry you. You don't have to beg. I wear a size seven in rings, and my favorite stone is a princess cut. Nothing too big, two or three carats will do." She giggled like a schoolgirl.

I rounded the island with our plates and sat at the bistro table in the large window. I loved sitting here looking out of the window at the beautiful scenery. The woods backed up to her home, and I couldn't ask for a more peaceful area to be in.

The sun beamed in the window, illuminating our skin, and the wind outside caused the trees to sway in the breeze.

"My parents are having Sunday dinner this afternoon at their home. Of course, we have been invited. I think it would be good for you to go if you are cool with that. I can pick my sister's brain too. Keisha is a detective for BlackWater PD, remember? Maybe she can tell us about anything new that has happened."

"Sounds good to me. I never turn down a chance for some good eats."

Switching gears, I got right to asking questions about her personal business. "So, Nia, how are you not spoken for? You are a beautiful woman with a great personality. Am I missing a red flag? Do you have ugly feet?" I said, dipping my biscuit in my grits then stuffing it in my mouth.

She threw her head back and roared with laughter. "I just don't have time or energy to deal with fragile egos. Once I let a man in on who I really am, things change. Who has time to keep dealing with that?"

I sat quietly watching her as she responded. "Some men can't handle being in a relationship with a strong woman. I can kick ass and pay my own bills. I would need a man that offers emotional intelligence and love, not just money and protection." I eyed her intently, taking it all in. I couldn't help but notice her fidget with the hem of her shirt under my gaze.

"What about you? I know about your ex, but that was a while ago. What red flag am I missing? Are you an aspiring rapper at forty or something?"

I chuckled, then tried to give her the mean face. "Ha-Ha. You have jokes. Ma'am, I am not forty, yet. No, I don't aspire to be a rapper either. I haven't been in a relationship since my ex. It really messed me up when everything was ripped from me because of her lies. Thinking we were going to get married and have a baby, all for that to be a lie."

I shook my head as the memories raced to the front of my recollection. "I don't really trust people. I want to love someone that's for me like I'm for them. When I love, I love hard. I can't wait to find someone to spoil, cuddle with, and love on."

I never broke eye contact with her as I continued to engage her heart with my words. I noticed her heartbeat picked up as I spoke about everything. The pulse point in her neck almost beat out of her body.

As I leaned in, I noticed her eyes drop to my lips. "We need to get ready for Sunday dinner," I said as I stood to my feet.

. I meant what I said about loving someone, but as much as I wanted to kiss her, I knew I wasn't ready to cross that line yet.

Walking away, I noticed Nia just sat there stuck. Her breathing had picked up slightly, then she closed her eyes tightly. I was having an effect on her in the worst way, and I loved being able to get in her head. She seemed to be on her game with a lot of things, but hopefully, I was the only one that could get to her.

We arrived outside of her parents' home later that evening. Nia didn't keep the casual look from earlier. She had her braids in a nice updo and a short, brown flowing dress with a dipped neckline. She paired her look with a nude high heel. Gone was the chill, comfortable woman from earlier, and in her place was a more polished and sophisticated look.

This was a complete change from earlier and all for a family dinner at home. The confusion must have shown on my face because Nia reached out to grab my hand as we walked up to the door. I shook my head to clear those confused thoughts out. Dressed for a fancy restaurant was crazy for a Sunday dinner at home with your immediate family. We could add that to the list of things the Grants were serious about.

"Hey, everyone!" Nia said as we walked into the home. I noticed a few of them were in Timothy's TV room. Her mom was still in the kitchen finishing up.

"Is that Nia? Finally, we can get star-" Shirley said, but was stopped by my presence. Her eyes dropped to our hands linked together with our fingers intertwined. My body tensed at her disapproving face. I didn't mind the little display of affection. In fact, I gripped Nia's hand tighter when she tried to release me. I didn't care if I wasn't Shirley's favorite, even though she didn't have a reason to dislike me. "You're here. And you brought... a guest," she said, hesitantly.

"Good seeing you again, Mrs. Grant!" I put on a cheerful voice then reached out my right hand to shake her hand, not dropping Nia's in the least bit. I could tell this made Nia feel a little on edge by how her body tensed. She watched us interact, intently.

"I'm sorry what was your name again?"

"Xavier, ma'am. I'm Nia's boyfriend."

This time, I released her hand and grabbed her around the shoulders into a hug. With the look on her face, you could have bought Nia for a nickel. Surprise was etched across her features.

Chapter 8

Nia

What. The. Hell? This is not happening. Why is Xavier being all extra right now?

"Boyfriend?" my mom and sisters said in unison. My dad just stood, leaned against the wall smiling. He was enjoying this a bit too much.

"Yes, everyone, this is my boyfriend, Xavier. We were reunited at the event. We really enjoyed each other's company that night and decided to take a chance on us."

He stood there smiling like a menace. Everyone seemed to be fine with it but my mom. I did not know what had her panties in a bunch, but she was not happy. Which was odd because she always harassed me to find a man. Now that I had one, kind of, she wasn't happy. Some people were just never satisfied.

Sitting at the massive wood dinner table quiet, I watched as my sisters eyeballed us. Mom sat at one end of the table, while Daddy sat at the other end. Jamilah sat across from Xavier with the twins while he and I sat side by side. Xavier talked and laughed with my dad while my mother scowled at them. She took a sip of her wine, looked at them over her glass, then cleared her throat. "So, when did this happen?" she said and waived her hand dismissively at both of us.

"Why are you moving so fast?"

I sat up straighter and put on my game face before I answered. I knew if Shirley was going to accept us as a real couple, I needed to really sell it. Then maybe she would let it go.

"We aren—"

In the middle of a laugh with my dad, Xavier's head whipped to my mom. His drink didn't even make it to his lips when he sat it back on the table.

He said, "I don't think we are moving fast." Xavier interrupted me while I was trying to defend us. "We just decided there was no need to play games. We are two adults looking for the same thing. We aren't getting any younger, so why beat around the bush?" he said so confidently then looked at me and winked. He sat back further in his chair then put his arm around the top of my seat. His presence and his cool demeanor under so much scrutiny calmed my spirit. I was able to snuggle under his arm as everyone talked at the table.

Jamilah jumped in, cutting through the deafening silence, and I couldn't be any more grateful. At this point, Mom was seething from the direct shutdown from Xavier.

"I hate that I didn't get a chance to meet you at the New Year's party, Xavier. What do you do? You give me quiet man, military vibes. Almost like Daddy,"she said as she swirled her hand in his face.

Xavier and my dad both chuckled. "I guess you can see, this is our dramatic one."

Jamilah scoffed and faked a shock and hurt expression.

"Yes, ma'am. I am ex-military, but now I am a serial entrepreneur. Working on a project now to bring grown and sexy for the mature crowd to this small town."

"So, you're unemployed?" my mom blurted out. You could hear a rat piss on cotton it was so quiet in the dining room. My eyes widened from the shock of the blatant disrespect. The look on my dad's face said a million words. First, his eyes bulged then narrowed on her.

"That's enough Shirley," My dad said with tight lips.

"What? I am just looking out for our daughter's future. How can he be a provider and protector when he is unemployed?"

She tried to look innocent after that statement. My mom had always been known to not bite her tongue, but this was beyond embarrassing. She had ruined a good night. It was time for us to go. I went to gather our plates and stand up, but Xavier grabbed my wrist, stopping me in my tracks.

"It's OK, baby, have a seat," he looked up in to my eyes and said. I sat my ass down. Looking over at my daddy for help, he just sat there drinking his whiskey.

"Since I left the military, I made it a point to not work for another soul or give my time and energy to build someone else's dream. I had a few real estate investments, and I had a few businesses back in California. So, I guess you can say I am unemployed since I sold them all, but I'm far from broke. I can provide and protect what's mine."

He said it so calmly and held eye contact with my mom as he let her know. He watched her a little longer after his response to see if there was more, but she was quiet. She got up abruptly, grabbed her plate, and left the dining room as if she was now cleaning.

The girls and I decided to clear the dining room as well. I needed to go ahead and get it out of the way. I knew once I walked in the kitchen, she was going to give me an earful. Jamilah stopped me in the hallway. "I like him for your stuck up ass. Maybe he can help you not let Mommy and Daddy run your damn life." She shrugged her shoulders then walked off.

It must have been something in the air because everybody was feeling some kind of way tonight. I would address that little comment she made, but I had bigger fish to fry. I knew my mom was heated about that little showdown, but honestly, she deserved it. She tried to put him on the spot and embarrass him, but things didn't work out like she planned. Daddy didn't even try to save her. By the time I made it in the kitchen, she was gone to her room. Good. I didn't want to deal with the fall out that came with this conversation.

My dad kept Xavier occupied most of the night. When it was time for us to leave, I thought I was going to have to break them up. They really bonded over whiskey and basketball. Xavier grabbed my hand and my keys, then walked us to the car. He was a damned good actor, even had me convinced a few moments tonight.

As he drove us back to my house, he silently gazed at me with those sexy eyes. They looked to be holding in so many emotions, so many questions. I wish I knew what he was thinking. Tonight was a lot. The displays of affection, the entertaining, and I knew he was still worried about our actual reason for doing all of this. He should be tired, but he handled it well.

Without thinking, I reached up and rubbed the back of his head as he drove. It felt natural to me to want to soothe him. The moan from his chest caused my panther to whine inside. She was absolutely taken by him. She had no understanding that this was not real and would end as soon as we found the people hunting his family. She wanted him. Hell, so did I. He looked over at me again, but this time, his eyes were heavy-lidded. If I kept stroking the back of his head, I might be in trouble.

I moved my hands back in my lap and apologized for over-stepping. He didn't mention it; he just kept driving. The rest of the ride was quiet as we both retreated into our heads to get lost in our thoughts. I went straight to my room when we made it home.

We worked tirelessly at the beginning of the week to try and uncover what we could about the people after his family. Wednesday evening, we sat at the dining room table going over the letters sent to Jerome when my phone rang.

"Hey, Daddy! What's going on? Do you have any new info about Jerome?"

"Hey, baby girl! No, but I do have a new target. We can't shut down shop just to help my friend. We still have people to drop and more money to be made."

As he went on about the assignment, I rolled my eyes. I was mentally drained and just wanted a bath and my bed. I still had to juggle my event clients, the onyx clients, and now... Jerome's mess.

Xavier watched as I finished the call. Breathing hard, I shared the news with him. "We are going to have to pause right here because I have a job at the casino in Miramar Isle tonight. Apparently, there is a regular at the casino who is forcing himself on the women workers. He harasses them then waits on them after their shift and attacks them. Women are coming forward about it, and the owner needs this threat neutralized. I need to start getting ready."

"You mean WE need to start getting ready. I'm not letting you go out and do this alone. Plus, I love seeing you in action. Why are you taking this job and not one of your sisters though? I can see in your eyes you are tired." Slumping my shoulders, I heavily exhaled.

"Since I am the lead huntress, it kind of all falls on me. The twins have the ability to do jobs, but we try not to involve them. You know Keisha is the detective, so she really can't, and Aaliyah is the peacemaker. She might want to have an intervention instead of taking them out. Daddy knows I get in and get it done."

"Hmm. Jamilah is an option, too, right?"

"Nooo... not really. She is our handler. Without her, we would be lost."

I couldn't go into the real reason why she couldn't. I couldn't exactly tell him she didn't have her panther yet to protect her if things got sticky or that there were panther shifters at all.

"Well, let's get ready then."

Standing, he headed to his room. I went up to my room and turned on some music before I hopped in the shower. When I walked into the living room, Xavier stood and gasped at what he saw.

I walked in with a knee-length, all black, sleeveless A-line dress with pockets. My black and red stilettos with spikes on the heels, that doubled as retractable weapons, set off the look. I decided on wearing a solitaire diamond necklace that acted as a camera as well for Jamilah. Since she had not had her first shift, we couldn't mind-link yet. We used a very small two-way communicator insert for the ear. Even if Xavier was all on me, he wouldn't even notice it. The look was simple, elegant, and classy. I wanted to spark interest, not draw too much attention that would make the target shy away.

Xavier didn't look too shabby himself. He chose to wear black slacks and a black Versace collared shirt with his diamond Cuban links chain. His facial hair was nicely groomed and framed those sexy lips just right. We could blend in as a regular couple looking to do some regular gambling.

"The plan for tonight is to get close to the target. Watch him in action and drop the poison in his drink. Plan b, if we don't have a window for that, I'll get him alone and take him out. We need to be discreet, so we don't cause any panic and bring heat to the casino," I said as we stood face to face. He took a step back, and his eyes roved over my body. I think he liked what was in front of him.

"After you, my lady."

We took his black Audi A6 and valet parked at the door. He walked over to my side, gave the valet his keys, then guided me inside with his hand at the small of my back. Walking into the casino, Jamilah found my target and gave me the next steps in my ear. I found him, and we decided to watch for a bit.

Xavier leaned into the side of my face, and with a low, sexy voice, asked, "Do you want something to drink?"

I cut my eyes to watch his sexy lips move. Heat rushed over my body at the deep timbre of his voice. Smiling, I nodded my head. We went to the bar on the side of the blackjack table where we kept eyes on the target. He was a middle-aged white man who looked to have a bit of disposable income based on his attire.

He was very flirty with the ladies, offering the dealer compliments and tipping generously. When the dealer didn't play much into his advances, he turned his sights on to the waitress coming around for drink orders. Jamilah kept up with everything from my necklace and told me we might have to go straight to plan b. She saw what I couldn't, and there was no window of opportunity to slip anything in his drink.

He ordered drinks but didn't drink much. As he went to tip, he would grab them by their wrists or around the waist to whisper in their ear, a little too handsy for my liking. I tapped Xavier on the bicep to tell him we needed to get closer.

Grabbing his hand, I led him over to the blackjack table. "Daddy, I want to play this one," I stated in a high-pitched, overly whiney voice.

His eyes lowered and darkened as he stared at me. "Maybe we can learn something from this big man right here."

I turned to my target and pouted, "Would you walk me through how to play this game? You seem to be doing well with it with all of those chips."

He smiled big and poked his chest out. He looked at Xavier like he was asking for permission. When Xavier nodded his head for him to proceed, that was all we needed. Got him! He was putty in my hands then. "Nice to meet you, I'm Karma!" I said sultrily with a raised eyebrow then extended my hand to shake his. "This is my boyfriend, John."

He looked shocked at my friendliness. I played the novice good girl role very well. Even though, I could beat his ass with my eyes closed. I won some, and I lost some. I kept ordering vodka and cranberries as we played.

I wanted him to think I was getting drunk even though it was hard for that to happen with shifters. We had to put away larger amounts for it to affect us like it did humans. I made sure to slow my wording as I talked to Xavier. I leaned over to his ear and loudly slurred out a whisper, "Going to the little girl's room. I'll be back."

As I stumbled away, I glanced back to see my table partner watching. Xavier's head was down looking at the table, so I winked and crooked my finger to instruct him to come with me. He met me in the isolated hallway to the bathroom.

I walked to him, then asked, "Do you want me?"

He grabbed me roughly. Pulling me closer by my butt, he started groping me and kissing my neck. Rubbing his back, I walked us further into the hall so that we were out of view of any cameras. I needed to hurry so I could stop this disgusting slob from touching me.

As our bodies were colliding with the men's restroom door, I lifted my leg up and wrapped it around him. I reached to pull a mini syringe from my garter under my dress. A quick jab of a lethal amount of potassium would put him down quickly and not show up in an autopsy to prompt an investigation. As his body started jerking, I yelled, "Oh my God! I think he is having a heart attack. Someone help!!"

He laid on the floor clutching his chest. The symptoms mimicked a heart attack. As workers rushed in to assist the man dying on the floor, I feigned distress. Walking back to the blackjack table, Xavier asked if I was good. Shaking my head yes, I asked, "You ready to go daddy?"

He chuckled. "Keep that daddy shit up, and it's going to be a problem."

Grabbing my hand, he led me to the car. The valet was pulling the vehicle up as we walked out.

Chapter 9

Xavier

I sat in awe as I watched the women of the Onyx work together to take down their target. Nia was in the zone as she listened to Jamilah communicate about everything in her ear. Dressed to kill, Nia had on a sexy dress and heels. We walked into a vibrant casino bustling with patrons, and it instantly overwhelmed my senses. Cigarette smoke and stale, recycled air prickled my nostrils. Complete opposite of the clean air in our foresty town. People were everywhere eager to give away their money to the slot machines. The tables were a little more sparse. Nia grabbed my hand and guided us to the bar. When we found the target sitting at the blackjack table, she turned on her character, and I think I fell in love.

Pulling me along like a toddler in a toy store, she eagerly led me to him.

"Daddy, I want to play this one," she stated to me, and I felt my pants tighten around my hips. She caught me off guard with that, and my body immediately reacted. "Maybe we can learn something from this big man right here."

She turned her body to him, then said, "Would you walk me through how to play this game? You seem to be doing well with it with all those chips," she flirted. Playing up that good innocent act, had me ready to risk it all on her.

Her target smiled big and poked his chest out. He then looked at me, his brain must have registered he needed to check with me first. In order not to blow her cover, I just nodded back, but I really wanted to break his neck. If he put his nasty ass hands on her, I might just lose it. He looked well off in quiet luxury pieces like that Jaeger-LeCoultre watch. Money could only buy materials, not morals. The things I had heard about his interaction with these women let me know he was morally bankrupt. Rolling my neck, I tried to keep it cool.

"Nice to meet you, I'm Karma!" she said in a sultry tone, then shook his hand. "This is my boyfriend, John." He was so entranced by her body that her name didn't even raise any red flags. Idiot!

Nia played this role through a few games and had me ready to get out of here to be alone with my thoughts. I was feeling way too much for Nia, and I needed to sort this shit out ASAP. Why was I feeling possessive of her? I wanted her smiles, her giggles, her experiences. This was supposed to be fake. Every confusing thought and feeling was very much real though.

She downed those drinks like a professional, but I have only ever seen her drink wine. I prepared myself to step in if she kept this up. This nasty man would take advantage of her if given the slightest opportunity. Nia stood up, catching our table partner's eye. He tried to watch her from the side, but I caught him gazing at her frame from the back. She leaned in close to my ear, her sweet scent enveloping my senses, and faked a whisper. Nia was making her move now. She said she was going to the restroom, and when I looked at her, to assess if she could handle it, she seemed alert. She wasn't a light weight at all with drinking, apparently. With a wink, she dragged her hand across my back and walked off toward the restroom area. I felt more confident in her execution now that I saw the alcohol hadn't impaired her functioning.

I kept my head down to pretend I was oblivious to what she was doing, I knew it was only a matter of time. Standing from the table, I pulled my phone out to call for our car. As soon as she returned, I needed to take my ass home. Not even five minutes later, there was a commotion, with screaming and employees running to that area. She walked back to me with immense eye contact, sashaying her hips and a look so innocent, she could fool a psychic. As she made it back to the blackjack table, I asked if she was good. She looked me square in my face and said, "You ready to go, daddy?"

I chuckled. "Keep that daddy shit up, and it's going to be a problem."

I grabbed her hand and interlaced our fingers. *Why did I do that?*

The feel of her soft, velvety skin was the perfect fit of her small hand in mine. As the valet pulled the car up, then opened her door, my body heated.

"I got it, man." I stopped in my tracks and shook my head. I didn't want another man opening the door for her. *What is going on?*

After I got her situated in the car, I walked around to the driver's side. I took that brief time to breathe in deeply.

We drove off from the casino, and I couldn't be happier that was done. The tension rolled off of Nia as she sat quietly in the passenger seat. My eyebrows drew together when I looked over to ask, "Are you OK? You seem tense. Did you get it done? Did he do something to you?"

She looked in my direction, but not directly at me. Her eyes were vacant. My chest constricted. She was uneasy. She had put herself on the line for a job, and something happened.

"I just need to get home and take a shower. He rubbed his grubby hands all over me, and I feel disgusting."

Heat shot through my body, starting from my toes. The leather on the steering wheel whined as I gripped it tighter in an effort to gather my emotions before my temper took over. Suddenly, my clothes were too tight, and I needed air. If he wasn't already dead, I would kill him with my bare hands.

I had no words to offer Nia. I was glad that's all that happened, but shit, that was too much. Reaching over, I grabbed her hand and interlocked our fingers again. She took in a deep breath and exhaled. Her body, once tensed, finally started to relax as she closed her eyes. Her breathing evened, and there was a light snore. I smiled, knowing she felt safe enough with me to let her guard down to sleep.

Sitting straighter in my seat, my thoughts drifted back to tonight. Nia to on a lot for her family, even at the cost of herself. Now, she was helping my family. She was amazing tonight, and I knew these jobs could take a lot out of you. As we pulled into her driveway, I decided not to wake her. I carried her up to her room and took off her shoes and placed her under her covers in bed. The overwhelming feeling to lay beside her with her head on my chest caused a lump in my throat as I looked down in her peaceful face as she slept.

After my shower, I laid in the bed and let my mind wander. Thoughts of Nia being my lady were heavy on my mind. She was selfless, loyal and an overall beautiful woman. With me, she wouldn't have to take on all of these jobs alone. Hell, with me, maybe her family would stop looking to her as the savior. I liked. Timothy, but he leaned too heavily on her for all the Onyx's needs. Her mom was way too critical of her as well. I wanted to shield her from the things that drained her.

My thoughts were on Nia until I drifted to sleep. She even took over my dreams. I saw her face under me as I eased more

81

of her burdens. I wanted to be it for her. Be the protector that she definitely needed to help her with boundaries and show her a life that wasn' just work and perfection.

The sun shining brightly and disrespectfully brought me from my sleep. Laying in this soft bed, I let the sun rays charge my tired body. I needed all of the Vitamin D I could get right now. My body was exhausted from all of the mental work this ordeal with my dad brought. My brain had been plagued with thoughts of who could be after my family, and now, another layer had been added to the loop—being with Nia. I hadn't even had time to deal with my business venture.

Dealing with all of this stuff with my dad and mentally sorting through it with Nia had me tired. I just wanted to lay here and stare out of this bedroom window. The beautiful forest backed up to Nia's home was relaxing. This girl had been heavily rotating through my thoughts. We got a little closer Wednesday night. The vibe was natural. It had been between us since we met again as adults.

The aroma of freshly brewed coffee hit me and gave me the push I needed to start my day. I got out of bed, dealt with my hygiene, then walked to her kitchen. Nia seemed to be in a much better headspace than last night. She stopped prepping breakfast and raised her eyes up in my direction. She stared with a glint in her eye. A lazy smile spread across her face when we locked eyes.

"Good morning and thank you for last night!" she said as she continued breakfast.

"Good morning," I replied sluggishly. There was no need to thank me for what I did last night, so I ignored that part. I drug my body to the island and sat in the bar stool to watch her work her magic in the kitchen. I scrolled silently on my phone as she cooked. Walking up to me, Nia sat the plate in front of me and placed her back against the island to search my face. I tried to ignore her presence since I knew she was about to get in my business.

"You look tired. Are you OK?"

Shaking my head, I let out a long exhale. "Just a lot on my mind has me needing some rest."

She leaned into my side and smiled up at me. "Well, let's take our food outside so we can soak up some sun. I always feel better after I connect with nature."

Sliding off the barstool, I followed her as she grabbed our drinks, and I took our food to the patio. We ate in silence, then she dropped a bomb on me.

"I need your help," she said as she sat up straighter going into business mode. "Before I took your family on as a client with Onyx, I had a retirement party for one of our fathers' friends. I need you to be my plus one and extra eyes for tonight. There may be another attempt on your family tomorrow night. This time, in person." She stared into my eyes as she delivered those words. Nia had picked up on a few things about me. She knew my family was my weakness.

My breathing stopped at her words. I was able to handle a lot, shit, I was in the military. We dealt with a lot of stuff thrown at us, but my family was one way to get me off my square. "Sure! Just tell me what you need me to do."

We spent the rest of the day setting up and going over security plans for my family. Tomorrow was the retirement party, and we needed to be ahead of the game now that we knew the target.

Friday evening, the tension in my shoulders had me ready to jump in a warm bath, and the event just started. I made it before the guests arrived and checked the perimeter of the building. Security was in the building for any major issues, but I was sitting back watching everyone else for more subtle threats. Nia was looking and smelling good as usual. Tonight, though, she seemed a little more relaxed with me. Even though she was busy hosting and putting out fires, she was a lot more at ease. Nia and I finally sat down during the dinner with our parents. As we enjoyed the conversation and live music, Nia stood to go check on something.

As I watched Nia walk away, my eyes landed on someone walking up to our table, and not just any someone –Alissa, my ex. My mom immediately recognized her and jumped up to greet her. They used to have a great relationship before we broke up. Alissa would call and check on my mom, or they would go shopping when my mom came to visit.

Our breakup saddened my mom because she looked at Alissa as the daughter she always wanted, but when I looked at her. I felt nothing. No anger. No love. I felt more annoyed because there was no reason for her to be here. Especially with Nia coming back any minute. I didn't want her to think that Alissa had any chance with me. After our time together and our day yesterday, Nia was the one I wanted. I couldn't allow Alissa to kill my chances before I told Nia how I really felt about her.

Chapter 10

Nia

Being at this retirement party with Xavier had me all giddy and feeling more into him than ever. His fine ass decided on a black suit with a crisp white button down. He brought a little ice out to rest on his wrist and in his ears. The diamonds made that crisp edge up stand out so bold against his chocolate skin. He always smelled edible, and tonight was no different. His presence brought out a lighter side of me that most people didn't see.

We had spent a great deal of time together, and I had learned to trust him. I trusted that I was safe with him. I trusted that he would keep his word. He hadn't given me any reason yet to not trust him. But I didn't trust the woman that just walked up to our table. Our parents were sitting around the table catching up with each other when a random woman walked up. She was a caramel-colored woman with wide hips and big lips, thick in all the right places. She was pretty and definitely interested in Xavier.

The Carters seemed to know her, and she didn't look like a threat. From the looks of things, whoever she was, Xavier wasn't happy to see her. All conversation had stopped, and all eyes were on the mystery woman that just walked up. My mom caught my eye and raised an eyebrow. She mind-linked me. Apparently, the guest of honor was a childhood neighbor of the mystery woman. That's all the info she had at the time.

Xavier's mom, Barbara, seemed to know her very well, and it made my shoulders tingle. I didn't like it... whatever that was over there. Instead of rushing back, I got closer to see what was going on. *Who am I becoming?*

I had never spied on a boyfriend, let alone a fake boyfriend. I had to admit, I was starting to feel things for Xavier. Shit! This was going to be terrible when he messed this up. I needed to get it together.

As I stood next to another guest for the party, I heard that it was his ex. *What? Why is she here? What does she want?*

Standing up straighter, I politely excused myself from the conversation and headed back to my table.

"Excuse me!" I said as she stepped back so could I slip back into my seat. Leaning into Xavier's side, he reached to put his arm around my shoulders. As I got comfortable in my seat, I lifted my head up to look in his eyes. He stopped glowering at her to look down at me with my lips poked out. He dropped his head and pressed his lips to mine in a sweet kiss. My eyes instinctively closed, and a moan rumbled from my throat. The world around us seemed to drop from existence. Parting from that kiss, this man had me hot and bothered. From the looks of it, the kiss affected him too. Breathing hard, he looked down into my face with a slight smirk on his lips.

"I'm sorry, did I interrupt something?" I turned my head in his ex's direction. The look on her face brought joy to my heart. There she stood, too stunned to speak. Everyone at the table sat in silence as this all played out. I knew what she did, and I didn't care at all for her feelings in this moment. Hopefully, she didn't think she would just walk her ass in here and pick up where they left off. Hell no! My panther wanted to rip her face off, but I think a little embarrassment would suffice.

"I just wanted to come over and speak," she said awkwardly. "It was good seeing you again, Xavier. Maybe we could catch up sometime. I'll be in town for a few more days."

Looking over to Xavier, he was not in the least bit interested in what she had to say. He was too wrapped up in cuddling with me at this table. I decided to play nice by sticking my hand out to introduce myself.

"I'm so sorry. Hi! I'm Nia, Xavier's girlfriend. Are you guys friends from Cali?"

"I'm Alissa, his ex-girlfriend, and Barbara's other child." She looked at Barbara, giggled, and shook my hand.

Feeling Xavier tense up beside me, I could tell our interaction was making him uncomfortable. This would be the perfect time to dance. Gabbing his hand, I pushed my chair back and led us to the dance floor. The jazz band was playing Sadé which was perfect for us to be close and talk. I wrapped my arms around his neck as he pressed his hard body against mine as we swayed. He smelled so sexy to me. I just wanted to lick the side of his neck. The leather and patchouli scent had me ready to climb him like a tree. That task was nothing for a panther. Whispering in his chest, I asked, "How are you feeling, seeing your ex here?"

He chuckled. "I thought it would bother me, but honestly, I couldn't care any less than I do now. I'm not worried about that girl."

His deep voice rumbled from his chest and relaxed me like nothing else could. It reminded me of the panther mating grumble. Xavier had his arms around my waist when he decided to lean down to meet my lips again. This time, it was no sweet, innocent kiss. He took my bottom lip into his mouth and gently sucked it. He licked the opening of my mouth then pushed his tongue inside. The moan that left my lips startled me. When he let me up for air, I was slightly dazed. I couldn't have imagined the softness of his lips and the taste of his tongue.

Breathily, I tried to gain my composure and said, "You are really enjoying yourself, I see." I giggled, staring up into his beautiful, brown cinnamon eyes. They were different, warmer... more intense.

"Too much, Nia. I want you. This isn't pretend anymore." My breath hitched as I stopped swaying and just searched his face for any deception. Could I do this with him? I needed time to think. I needed to get out of here for a few minutes. I began looking around for an escape. As I scanned the room, I saw my father at the table watching us. In true Timothy fashion, he sat with an Old Fashion in hand and a smirk on his face. If I didn't know any better, I would swear he set this up.

Rushing off to the bathroom, I needed to get myself together. What did this man just say to me? I rested my hands on the sink counter and closed my eyes to breathe in and relax my nerves. *I'm not ready. Isn't this what I wanted?*

So, what was my problem? As I was trying to talk myself in to going back out there, the doors burst open. The mirror in front of me confirmed who it was...Alissa. Placing on my fakest smile, I noticed she didn't return the gesture but was walking toward me with an attitude.

"Don't get comfortable. He will be back where he belongs soon. I let him have his space for a while, but that's done now. I miss that dick and them pockets. I plan to ride both, reeeaal soooonn." She chuckled and walked into a stall.

My heartbeat picked up as I tried to calm my breathing. There was no way I was letting that happen. Xavier was too good of a man to fall back into that trap. Even if we didn't get together, what kind of friend would I be to let him fall back into whatever spell she had him under?

The toilet flushed, and she walked out to wash her hands. As I walked to the door, I wanted to leave her with something. "Ma'am, focus on finding your baby a daddy. Xavier is already taken, and trust, I won't be foolish enough to give him up anytime soon. Unlike you, I'm not a hoe."

I threw my head back and walked out the door laughing from my belly.

A few steps out the door, I ran into the man I was looking for leaning against the wall. His face was scrunched, and his eyebrows drew close together. He stood up straight and grabbed me as I approached. "Are you OK? What did she say to you? I saw her go in after you, but I couldn't catch her to stop her."

"I know you're not worried about me. You should be worried for her safety."

His shoulders dropped as we both laughed loudly.

"You right. What did she say? She has a slick mouth, so I know she said something."

"Yeah, that she missed your dick and your pockets."

I narrowed my eyes at him as he winced from my words. I crossed my arms over my chest in a fake attitude. Instead of speaking, he bent down, wrapped his arms around my waist and placed his face in the crook of my neck. His kisses started out slow, then they turned into him licking and sucking my neck until we were interrupted.

We both stood up straight and gathered ourselves. He had me out here acting like a high school girl under the bleachers. As

Alissa walked by, she made sure to stop with one last message for Xavier. "My number hasn't changed when you get tired of playing in the kiddie pool."

"I don't like to swim in public pools, too much access. I like things a little more... exclusive. Where the wetness is just for me."

My eyes bulged out of my head at his comment. He grabbed my hand and led us back out where the party was wrapping up. The night was perfect. We got a chance to put his ex to rest, and his family was safe.

The night turned out to be a regular one, thankfully. Unlike we originally thought, it was a good time with both of our families. That led me to believe that we were dealing with something else entirely, or they were watching closely for the next opportunity to strike.

Heading home, the drive was quiet, but my thoughts were loud. Was he serious, or was it just a show? As he pulled my Escalade into the driveway, there were a lot of unanswered questions between us. Silence took over as we unloaded the car then went in our separate directions to our rooms.

Laid in bed, my brain worked overtime to make a decision. I wanted Xavier, but what about everything else... like my panther. Could he deal with a girlfriend and the issues with his dad? I listened for any movement coming from his room and realized I wanted to be under him. Maybe we could go slow. Getting out of bed, I grabbed my robe to cover my favorite rose gold nighty.

It always made me feel sexy, so I made sure to keep different colors in rotation. Barefoot, I tiptoed to his room to see him, half naked, laid on the bed with his arms behind his head. He seemed to be watching TV, but as soon as I walked to his door, his eyes were on me. Biting his lip, he stared at me with lidded eyes.

Darkness covered the room, and the only light was from the television show. Plopping down on his bed, he sat up to figure out the reason for my presence.

Taking a deep breath, I looked at him and said, "I trust that you will take care of my heart."

He silently stared into my soul. He leaned in slowly, and his beautiful brown eyes came closer and looked down to my lips. He inched closer and pressed his big, soft lips against mine. They felt like pillows of heaven. A soft moan escaped from my mouth, and at that moment, I knew I was safe with this man. He wrapped his strong arms around my waist as his tongue caressed mine. My body instinctively fell into submission. This was all foreign to me. No man had made *me* feel safe and cared for. I was this big panther shifter that could physically protect herself. The safety I needed was emotional.

"Now, I don't give this dick to just anybody. Please understand, there is no changing up on my end, and you are mine to have, if we go any further." He arched a brow. "Can you handle that?"

I nodded so hard, my brain rattled, but the nervous squeak that slipped out totally betrayed me. He quickly swooped my body under him, holding his weight with his elbows.

"I need your words, baby."

"Yes, I can handle it," came out as a whisper so soft, if he wasn't hovered over my trembling body, I doubt he would have heard it. My panther was excited to have him here. It had been a while since we had a partner. She watched at the surface as he laid on top of me. Our hearts beat fast. The excitement of taking this next step had me wetter than Niagara Falls.

"Can I taste you? I know that thing is as sweet as it smells."

"Yes, please." His warm breath caressed my face, taking his time sliding down my body. He slapped my hand away when I went to take the nighty off but reached down and pulled it to the side.

"That pretty goodness is glistening for me." He reached down and grabbed himself through his sweats. His skin glowed, rich with gold undertones above me as he enjoyed his meal.

Kissing my inner thighs, I let out a whine reminiscent to a cat purring. He was taking his time with it, and it was driving me crazy. I grabbed his head and rubbed over the waves as he glided his tongue over my sensitive bud. Up, down, and all around my clit, his tongue ventured, exploring all of me.

My back arched as he blew on my clit and sucked on my bundle of nerves. He worked me over too good. "Do you like that?"

He ran his hands over my heated frame and grabbed at my breasts to roll my hardened nipples between his fingertips.

Turning the heat up on me just a tad more, he ran his tongue on my opening and swallowed my wetness.

"Shit!" I yelled out.

He was like a fat man with cake. Gripping my thighs, he raised my ass in the air to take a taste of the forbidden hole. Baby, we getting nasty today. I grabbed at his wrists and whimpered as he pleasured me, oh so sweetly.

He took a step back to admire the sloppy wetness he created when I looked at him with my sex dazed eyes and grabbed at his jeans. My eyes were low, and my hands were free. I reached under his shirt to glide my hands over his abs. With physical touch being his love language, I knew he was in heaven. I slid his jeans and boxers down and spanked him on the ass.

"Watch out now." He chuckled.

I came face to face with the big monster waiting to meet me.

Grabbing his shaft with my left hand, I grabbed and massaged his balls with my right hand. I could barely wrap my hands around that python. Giving it a squeeze, I admired the veins covering his dick. The thick chocolate rod looked good in my hands, especially with this new French tip manicure. I held it up and kissed down the back of his dick and licked his sack. Running my tongue along that main vein up to the head, I tasted the pre-nut and smiled. "I like the way you taste."

When I took his head in my mouth, he hummed in pleasure. I was taking my time devouring him. As I bobbed my head up and down, he wrapped his fingers in my braids.

Taking a fist full of my braids, he pulled my head back. Looking me in the eyes, he said, "I want to be inside of you."

I sat on the bed with no idea how this would go. The look in his eyes told me things were about to be turned up a notch. He pulled out a condom from hispants pocket as he continued to stare into my eyes. I laid back, watched him sheath himself, then climb on top of me. I grabbed his face and brought his lips to mine. His lips were so soft and sweet like cognac, I didn't want to let go. He lined himself up at my entrance as he continued to kiss and suck on my lips. Pushing in slowly, I moaned against his lips. This felt perfect. The stretch had me drenched. That feeling hurt so good. .

Long, deep strokes had me panting and scratching at his back. He yanked his shirt over his head, I felt all his hard muscles under his smooth skin glide across mine. I pulled him closer so that more of his weight was on me and wrapped my legs around his waist. His low rumble and grunts had me about to lose it. I wasn't the only one affected since he had to get out of it for a second to compose himself.

"Head down, ass up, darling!" Sliding back inside, he threw his head back and realized this was a mistake. I took control, started throwing it back on him, and all he could do was hold on for the ride. He was now the audible one and didn't care who heard. This was heavenly. As we both climaxed, all he could do was shake his head in disbelief as our breathing returned to normal.

He laid on his back and pulled me to his chest for a few minutes after he got us cleaned up. I didn't mind being engulfed in his scent as we both drifted off into a sex coma.

Back to business, I sat in the middle of the living room, with all the info I had about the attacks on Xavier's family. My glasses were on and my hair in a messy bun while I intently ran through everything I was able to pull up on the Carter family, biting my nails. My favorite reality TV show played in the background.

From what I was able to find out, right now, I think it is someone from Jerome's past. But WHY?!

"What is Jerome into?" I whispered to myself.

It was a beautiful day with the sun shining bright. The wall of windows in my home allowed the sun to beam directly inside and bring warmth into the large living space. Wearing thot gear, Xavier walked in wearing grey sweatpants, leaned down, and pecked me on the lips. "How long have you been at this? I see you have your favorite show on. I hate these reality shows. Why do you love them so much?"

It took me a few minutes to look up and acknowledge Xavier. Did he just kiss me? Having a man was all still new territory for me.

"Not long. I just wanted to get a head start on looking at all the evidence. We have to see if I can make some kind of connection. Since we can't bring my sisters in on this project, it's just us. Jamilah is really the brains behind our projects and solving these types of issues. I have to get this to keep your family safe and keep our name in good standing. My dad has a lot riding on this. And if you must know, I love these shows because the women are so free and unapologetic."

I tapped the pen on myleg, wondering how to proceed. I couldn't let my dad down and miss anything. We couldn't afford to make a mistake.

I noticed Xavier was just standing there staring at me. "What?" He turned his head slightly to the right and looked confused.

"Why do you care so much about the family reputation? I noticed your decisions are heavily dictated on how it affects your family and the reputation. You have mentioned this before."

"You wouldn't understand. I am the oldest girl. I have to take care of everyone and be everything to everybody. My dad wanted boys, but he got me. A girl. The first born was a girl. Then they kept trying, and we were all girls. I am in line to take over the Onyx Hunt, and those are big shoes to fill."

"You don't want it?"

"It's not that. It's just...some days, I want to be...free. Just want to be...Nia."

Xavier sat beside me and crossed his legs.

"What does being Nia entail?"

"X, it's too much to go into. Think of it as an onion. I am not just a pretty face."

"Yeah, I noticed that since we have been spending time together. I think you are so much more, and I want to peel the layers back. If you let me."

"I think I'm ready to let you."

I smiled hard when he moved in closer to kiss my lips.

"I like it when you call me X."

I looked up at him with a shy smile.

"Makes me feel all powerful and stuff."

He kissed me again. Maybe I could trust him with my secret. He seemed to be a good guy. My panther was anxious to get out and run. This case, and now this man... they were driving me crazy. This was going to be an issue. I needed to get a way for a few minutes.

"I am going out to take a walk. I need to think, then we can go to the Onyx to put our heads together with my dad."

As I walked out the back door, I noticed X standing in the window. I needed to get out of his line of sight so I could shift into my panther and run some of this off. Walking further into the woods, I decided now was a great time.

My bones cracked, and my body contorted as I shifted into my other form. A large, jet black panther with golden eyes now in the place of where my human form once stood. The wind in my hair and the beautiful sounds of the trees swaying calmed me immediately. Flowing streams of water allowed my panther to stop in her tracks and lay on the bed of grass.

The stress of a new chapter with a man, exposing my secret, and being the real me around him. The same man who was in danger, who I must protect, who had clouded my thoughts since we met. Being in nature always eased my panther's mind. This ease caused a tonal flutter deep in my chest as peace took over my body.

Xavier was walking through the woods yelling my name when I realized he was only about five feet away from me. My neck snapped up when I heard my name. I couldn't shift back at this moment—I might scare him. I just got this man, I didn't want to lose him already. He stopped dead in his tracks when he noticed me. We locked eyes, and I noticed a twitch of recognition on his right side.

What is he thinking?

I got to all fours and slowly glided toward him while he was still stuck in shock. I circled his stiff body and smelled his anxiety bleeding from his pores. I wanted to show him that I would not harm him, so I rubbed my body against his leg. My large, formidableframe was so overpowering, he stumbled.

"Hey! Don't hurt me. I was just out looking for my girlfriend. I know she is out here. Can you help?"

The tonal flutter came from my chest again, and I felt content with his presence.

"Nia is out here alone. I can't stay and play today. I have to find her and make sure she is OK. Maybe I will see you again soon, pretty girl."

I decided to wander off so that I could shift and get back to the house. X walked further into the woods calling my name before he turned and headed back in that direction. When I emerged arranging my jogger pants, so he had no room to question me, I saw him in the window on the phone. I hoped he did not cal for help. I started a light jog up to the door and heard him speaking with his dad.

"Hey! I'm back."

X rushed to me and grabbed me in a big bear hug. His heart was beating extremely fast, and I noticed a slight tremor when he grabbed my arm to look in my face. "Are you OK?"

His eyes were staring deep into my soul, and I saw something I had never seen before in them. I closed my eyes and nodded while I took in his strong arms. I allowed myself to become engulfed in his warm and woody scent. He felt like home.

"I just had the most interesting experience outside; I went looking for you in the woods. I ran across the biggest most beautiful panther ever, relaxing by a stream on accident. She didn't attack me or anything, it was weird.

"She felt... familiar. Those eyes...reminded me of yours. Beautiful, almond like, and captivating."

He paused for a moment. "Any way! Let's go get brunch. We both could use a break."

I didn't say a word, but I was surprised my facial expression didn't give me away. I had to tone my eyes down. I was sure he would keep talking about it, but nothing he said was negative. He had a great encounter with my panther, and my heart smiled that he didn't reject her. He seemed to like the experience.

"A panther? Wow! That's crazy." He was so astonished. "Brunch sounds good. Give me about thirty minutes to get ready."

With a wide grin, I ran to my room to get ready. Our first date as an official couple, for real this time. A squeal left my lips as I got myself together. Once my edges were laid and I was dressed to impress, I rushed back into the living room. Biting down on a smile, I walked in, and X was there waiting on me. He looked edible and smelled even better. That sun-kissed, rich brown skin glowed under his hunter green button down and brown slacks.

We walked into *Tasty South,* a nice little brunch spot in Miramar Isles, about thirty minutes outside of Blackwater Bay. The weather was nice, and the girlies were dressed to impress. The seating outside was packed, and the DJ was grooving. I wanted mimosas and vibes, plus they had the best catfish and grits in Miramar.

"So, I was going over your dad's bank accounts and noticed there were some big deposits, but nothing about them were consistent. Can you reach out to him today and ask about them? That may help us get one step closer to the WHY and possibly the WHO in all of this?"

The waitress came over, and I ordered my mimosa and catfish, fried hard, and grits with cheese. I noticed X really watching me after I asked about those accounts. He must have been really thinking about those deposits. "What's on your mind?"

"I hope my dad isn't on anything funny with these deposits. I know he has gotten caught up with other women before, and I hope that's not the case this time. My mom will be devastated."

Deposits were weird instead of withdrawals, though. Why would women be paying him? I know Xavier's daddy not slanging it for pay? This might be a worse discovery for X. His dad selling his body for money instead of paying women for sex.

Chapter 11

Xavier

After Nia's potential discovery, I sat up straight and took in a deep breath. I had no words. Could my dad be caught up in something illegal? He was such a strait-laced guy when he was in the military, except for messing around with other women. Was he back messing with different women again? I really hoped not. What could possibly be the issue now that would make him do something so stupid as to get caught up with the wrong people?

Sitting there getting lost in Nia's golden-brown eyes, I realized she seemed so carefree in this moment. She didn't have to be perfect in every way with me. She didn't have to watch a reality show to feel like she was living through them. I wanted to see her experience more of this softer life. I could tell she needed someone to make her feel safe to let go and relax. Her parents put so much pressure on her to be so picture perfect that she couldn't live how she wanted. I would make sure as long as I was around, my baby could experience, what they say, a "soft girl" life. Changing the topic from my dad, I wanted to know more about Nia.

She sat her second mimosa down and straightened her spine. Her eyes glossed over as if she was in a trance. She stated, "I want to be loved for every part of me. No switching up. I want to be in love with my person and have babies. Now, don't get it twisted, I love what I do, but what's so wrong with having it all?"

The waitress kept bringing over mimosas as we talked. As she sat there and poured her heart out to me, the need to give her everything she wanted and needed, grew inside of me.

"Nothing wrong with having it all, but can you handle surrendering to someone that wants to give you the *all*?"

As we sat in silence staring at each other, she cleared her throat and finished a few more mimosas. For some reason, I wanted to be the man to give her all her heart's desires. Show her that life shouldn't be so serious all the time. Show her she could be free to be her best self.

Wrapping up brunch, I paid our tab and was ready to head out. "Let's go, drunk woman, before you start twerking on the table. You know how women get after brunch. We should probably meet our dads at Onyx to discuss these bank account deposits."

I grabbed her hand as we walked toward the door. A group of ladies started twerking and chanting, aye!

Nia giggled as I chuckled and shook my head. That shit was contagious; we needed to walk faster. We walked out laughing, and soon as we crossed the threshold of the door, her body became stiff as a board. The hairs on her arm raised, and I noticed goosebumps appear.

"What's wrong baby girl? You making me nervous. Do you see someone?"

Looking around wildly, she shook her head. "No, something is off though. I can feel it. I don't know what it is, but let's just go to the car. You drive."

We walked briskly across the street to the parking lot. Nia picked up the pace as we crossed rows one and two. She ducked behind a large SUV to get to her car. She went to her side, looking around, and I walked to my side. As I opened my door, a shot was sent through my driver side door window. We were sitting ducks in the wide-open space with only cars to hide behind.

"Get down!" she yelled and grabbed her barretta. "Shit, shit, shit! I should have seen this coming."

Running to her side of the car, I knew we needed to get out of there, but getting in the car would make us sitting targets. Nia took a few shots in the direction the first shots came from. "There was no way you would have known this was going to happen, baby. Don't be hard on yourself. We are OK. Let's get to the Onyx so we can put our heads together."

"I will cover you. Head north so we can jump in a Chariot." I was grateful for those years of training the Grant girls had to endure. This type of knowledge was saving our ass. When the Chariot, the ride share company, pulled up behind a building two streets over, we jumped in with the quickness.

The Chariot ride to the Onyx was a welcomed silence but loud inside. My mind was spiraling out of control. These thoughts were so loud, I was unaware when we made it to our destination. Nia and I walked into the Onyx prepared to get some answers. It seemed that whoever was after my dad would get to him by any means necessary, and that included using his family and friends. But WHY? What could he have done, or what was he currently doing to create such an enemy? Someone wants him DEAD.

Staring off into space, Nia caught me stuck in my thoughts again. She had this pained look of empathy, but what looked almost like yearning. In the midst of this chaos, she felt something special for me. That was more than my last girlfriend. She didn't care much about my pain. She cheated, got pregnant, and then lied about the paternity. Shaking my head to bring me back to the chaos in front of me, I saw my dad trying to look innocent and confused. He knew something.

I needed to get back to my house for a few things that might give us a few more clues. "Nia, I need to go back to my house to get my camera. The thought just popped in my head that whoever is after my family might be closer than we think. Since I am always the photography guy for our family events, I want to go get my camera and look through some pics. You can stay here while I run over there and grab it. I can take a Chariot and come right back."

She was not excited about this idea at all. I could tell based on her hesitation to speak and her mean side eye. "Look woman, I will be OK. Did you forget I was trained in one of the best military branches in the world? They don't want it with me."

I laughed and tried to lighten the mood by hugging and kissing on her neck. I wanted to do this on my own so that I could think. I needed to wrap my mind around a new life with this beautiful woman who actually wanted to be with me.

How was I going to gain her trust? I knew she was hiding something. Those walls were built higher than the Eiffel Tower. If we were going to move forward and have a successful relationship, she needed to trust me. She mentioned men switching up on her once they found out something. I don't know about this news that she is hiding— that she believes will cause me to switch up on her, but I have to make her feel secure in me riding with her no matter what. Then, my damn dad. Unfortunately, whatever we uncovered, I believed it was going to alter everything in our family. I could feel it in my bones.

"OK. I know you don't need me protecting you. But understand, every Superman needs to know that there is someone willing to ride for him just as hard. You don't have to do this alone," she said this as she stood in my face and looked me square in the eyes, fixing my shirt. I looked down into her beautiful, golden-brown eyes taking it all in. Feeling the love from her words let me know my heart was in trouble. I needed to solve this mess with my dad ASAP, so it didn't interfere with us.

The Chariot ride pulled up a few streets over from the Onyx warehouse. I checked the app to confirm the ride and got in. The driver seemed perfect, not wanting to talk, the AC blowing cold and the old-school music not too loud. That was until I noticed he kept watching me in the rearview mirror. Maybe he was just trying to keep an eye on me like I was with him. Where was his GPS?

"Yo homie, this is not the way to the address I put in the app?"

"Yes, I am taking a detour because of construction."

"Naw, it wasn't any construction scheduled for the area. Man, what the fuck goin' on?"

Shit, I left my pistol at the warehouse. Nia was going to kick my ass when I got out of this. The driver must have read my body language and knew I was planning to jump from the car, when he sped up. Racing through the area adjacent downtown, we zipped past several industrial warehouses. I noticed the area was more desolate, and my options were now grim.

We pulled into a parking lot where we were met by a group of men. A tall black man came out from the shadows. He wore what looked to be an expensive Italian suit, being flanked by what looked like two big gorillas. I guess he took his protection serious and was worried about little ol' me. I didn't have a choice but to get out and face my fate. He stood straight with his hands clasped behind his back. "Mr. Carter! Welcome. My name is Shadow. We have much to discuss. Please come in."

As I walked into this abandoned looking warehouse, I remembered my training; watch your surroundings and remember the exits. In the event you had the opportunity to make a run for it, you needed to know your exit route. We passed three doors on the right and two on the left before we entered the interrogation room fully equipped with...a metal chair. The walls were gray, and there was only one overhead light available. I didn't think we would be doing much talking. Maybe just me.

"So, Mr. Carter. Where is your daddy hiding? We have a bone to pick with him. Call him."

"If I get him here, then you will just kill both of us. What is the motivator for me to call him?"

"My plan was not to cause you any harm, Mr. Carter. You are simply a means to lure him to me. Now, if you need some motivation, I think I have that covered."

Snapping his fingers, those two burly gorillas walked into the room as he walked out.

One yanked me out of the chair, and the other went to wailing on me. Shit! I needed to fight back, or I wouldn't make it out of here. As they were flinging my body like a rag doll, I grabbed the metal chair and started swinging. Apparently, I hit one of the big back bears across the head because suddenly, I was no longer being held down. I knew I could take the last one out myself. That chair was my best friend as I went to work on the second guy. He caught me with a few shots to the ribs. I just kept working on his head until he collapsed. I was so thankful I paid attention on the way inside. I bolted down the hallway, adrenaline had me ready for whatever, at this point. I needed to get back to my girl before things really hit the fan.

I sprinted toward the exit. Almost there. Just a few more steps. Suddenly, Shadow stepped out from a dark corner. My eyes ballooned, with one punch. He shook my jaw and caused me to see black spots. My head hit the ground hard, and everything went black.

Nia... I'm sorry. I should have listened.

Chapter 12

Nia

"**S**omething isn't right. I can feel it, Daddy."

I paced back and forth in the meeting room at Onyx Warehouse. My thoughts ran rampant. The beautiful yellow and white chamomile plant in the corner wasn't working at all to calm my nerves. I had called Xavier's phone multiple times with no answer. I sent texts, and they were all unread. I couldn't find his location. Again, that was a Jamilah thing. Bringing my sister in on this was looking more like a better idea. This would probably be solved by now if she were involved.

"Give him some time. He was trained by the best. If anything happens, he will be able to get away or contact us," my dad said.

His tone said he was calm, but the look on his face wasn't very convincing. He knew in his heart something was off as well as I did. I guess he was trying to be optimistic to keep me calm. It wasn't working at all. My panther wanted to go and find him, save him. She fell in love when they met in the woods. He took to her so well. He was not afraid, and she was able to be calm around him. She wanted to claim him immediately, but I had yet to even tell him about her.

My heart was hurting from the possibility of what was happening to him. A lumped formed in my throat. I paced the floor and knew I couldn't just sit around and wait. Jerome just sat there looking stupid. He knew this was his fault.

"Jerome, tell us what is going on? Your son is missing. Now is not the time to keep secrets."

My hands shook as my voice elevated. I would kill Jerome myself if Xavier was killed and he could have prevented it.

Jerome jumped from his seat aggressively, sweating. "I swear I have no idea what is going on. I hate this just as much as you do. Do you think I want my son out there in harm's way because of me?"

He paced back and forth, biting his bottom lip. Maybe he was telling the truth. His scent didn't give off deception but anxiety and...guilt.

My heart has never felt this way about anyone outside of my family. This man had come into my life and inserted a sense of peace and acceptance I had never felt. My parents wanted me to be more of what they wanted. He wanted me to give him me, unapologetically and freely. This was what I had always wanted. My brain was just holding me back. It's too soon. He would reject me once he knew about my panther. My heart wanted him. No, *needed* him.

I had to do something. Maybe I could trace his steps from his apartment. My heart loved him. I...loved him.

"Dad, I am going to X's apartment to see if I can trace his steps. Maybe I can find...something."

Scenting him should get me the info I needed. Jerome needed to go home and stay by the phone.

My panther's anxiety was through the roof with the need to find him. We needed to run to his house. It would be faster and help alleviate some of this pent-up anxiety. I shifted as soon as I hit the back door of the warehouse. Topping my speeds in the nineties, I was determined to save him by any means. Sleek, shiny obsidian fur gleamed from beside me. The coat appeared almost liquid, like black silk stretched over coiled muscle. Silver eyes, sharp and luminous, standing out against the darkness of its fur like twin moons. My dad. His presence was what I needed to ground me in this moment.

"Hey, babygirl! I wasn't going to let you go at this alone. I can see how much you care about him," my dad mind-spoke to me as we ran through the deep, quiet woods surrounded by tall trees high above filtering sunlight. Moss clung to trunks and stones, soft and velvety beneath my paws. The consistent rumble of my paws pounded on the ground in sync with the beating bass drum in my chest.

My body screeched to a halt when we reached the edge of the woods facing Xavier's home. Quiet. No movement out of the norm. Sniffing hard in the air, I picked up on that amazing scent I had been missing these last few hours. The scent was very weak, but it was there. With how faint it was, I doubted he even made it to his home. My dad and I locked eyes. The unspoken silence said it all. We were thinking the same thing. My dad and I walked to the front door and looked through the window. Inside, nothing seemed out of place.

"Dad, let's use his scent to see where he may have gone. Based on his scent, he went east. I didn't see signs of a struggle, and his car is still here. He may have taken a Chariot, but who knows? He may have thought he took a Chariot. That ride could have taken him anywhere."

Without saying a word, my dad gave steady but comforting eye contact. He knew time was ticking. The more time passed, the harder it would be to find him.

As soft, warm hues of orange, pink, and purple, spread across the sky, we arrived at a warehouse where Xavier's scent was the most potent. "Dad, he has to be in there. How are we going to get him out? There is no movement inside that I can see from here."

"We will have to sit and watch to see if there is a way inside. I saw a guard walk around the back and another guard went inside. Looks like he was being relieved."

Laid in the woods, I took on my shadow form to blend into the darkness. The silence of the woods set the stage for our attack. I noticed every hour on the hour a guard walked around the back, and the one from the back went inside. The place was only lit directly above the doors. "We need to make our way to the back and take out that one guard and wait for the inside guard to come to us. That is our ticket in," I said and pointed in their direction.

Plans made. Time to execute. Dad and I stalked toward the back of the warehouse slowly as to not cause any alarm. Dad shifted back to his human form and took out the guard with one swift blow to the back of the head. We drug his body into the woods, stole the uniform, and were back at the post within ten minutes as to not miss the next shift change.

Dad decided he would go in uniformed to get a closer look and leave the door open so my panther could sneak in when it was time. He mind-spoke to me about the happenings.

"Soon as you walk in, there are rooms on both sides. I think they are holding X in the third door on the left, coming in from the back door. It's pretty bad in here. There is blood on the walls in one of the rooms. Looks like someone was interrogated and tortured there."

My steps faltered at his words. Shallow breaths took over as my chest constricted. Could that be Xavier's blood?

"There are guards huddled by the front two rooms. We needed to create a distraction. I can shift and have them come out, then you slip in. Don't shift back into your human form until we are in the clear; you may not need to at all," Dad continued.

"Got it." Then I heard a loud boom from the back of the warehouse. Dad launched a branch to the back door, and when the guards came out to investigate, he interacted with them for a distraction. I slipped right into the back and found X laying in a corner battered and bruised. Jumping up to press down on the handle, I pushed the door open with my body. X jumped when he heard the door creak open. My panther slowly walked in toward him and nuzzled his shoulder. He was alive. Gratefulness rushed through me. He gasped when he finally looked up at me. Then there it was again, recognition. He looked deep in my eyes.

In a weak whisper, Xavier said, "Hey, pretty girl. Are you the one from Nia's house? H-How?"

Giving him another nudge and swinging my head toward the door, I hoped he got the message.

He hesitated. "Do you want me to go with you?"

I just looked in his one good eye until he stood up. Turning to walk back toward the door, I noticed he moved slow. He was badly beaten and limping.

"Dad, we are on our way out the back, but X is moving pretty slow. They beat him pretty bad. Can you lure them closer to the front or to the woods?"

As we approached the door, I heard footsteps behind us. When I turned to see who it was, a guard was launching toward Xavier. In an instance, I was on his ass. A roar came from my panther as she jumped to protect her mate. My panther would guard him with a fierceness since he had won her heart in the woods that day. He crashed to the ground with a hard thud as I sank my teeth into his neck, vicious and quick.

As I worked on the guard, Xavier kept pace to the door. Slow and steady until the chaos was behind him. We escaped the warehouse, ran to the edge of the woods, and waited until my dad caught up. My dad stood still with his nose pointed in the air. He had scented something but said nothing about it. The confused look on his face made me want to ask questions.

He nudged X then kneeled to help him on his back. X huffed and groaned but eventually made it on my dad's back in order to keep the pace. I knew we could no longer keep this secret. Once he recovered, I knew he would have questions of why two panthers were helping him escape. How could that happen... if he remembered anything. Those bruises on his head looked pretty bad. Whoever was in charge of this operation was a professional. They had definitely had a hostage or two, but they were no match for the panthers.

Chapter 13

Xavier

I had gotten my ass kicked, and I needed to find a way out of here. Eyes closed, I listened for any movement. Nothing. The hum of the light bulb and the air conditioner lulled loudly. Opening my eyes, I stilled my body and tried to look around my area. Pain shot through my head when I turned it as I focused my eyes through my blurred vision. My brain felt as if it had been squeezed with this bright overhead light. Groaning through my attempt to sit up, I realized I was alone. I needed to get out of here.

"H-hey! Hey! Alright. I'll call him!" I hoarsely yelled out to whoever would listen.

Hopefully, that was enough to get them to come in here. Nothing. Guards walked up and down the halls talking. They ignored my cries for help. Not even a twitch in my direction. I counted about five in rotation. I wasn't cuffed or tied down.

Amateurs. Thinking of a masterplan to escape was halted when I heard a thunderous sound from the back of the warehouse.

"I hope that's my ride."

I knew Nia and her dad wouldn't just leave me, I hoped. Mentally preparing to push my battered and bruised body for an escape, I closed my eyes. As I mustered up strength to stand, the door creaked opened, and the biggest cat I had ever seen stood against the door. With even only one good eye, I saw the beauty of the imposing presence of such a massive animal.

Gasping in disbelief, there it was again. The familiarity. The bright golden glint in the deep eyes of this cat looked so familiar. This couldn't be the same one from the woods at Nia's house. The cat stood by me and nuzzled my shoulder. She looked deep in my eyes. In a weak whisper, I said, "Hey, pretty girl. Are you the one from Nia's house? H-How?"

She stepped closer, nudging me with a silent urgency, then flicked her gaze toward the door an unspoken command to follow.

"Do you want me to go with you?"

She just stared at me until I rose to my feet. Creeping toward the back door, the majestic creature glanced at me limping, and it was as if she felt sorry for me. This was crazy. I must be dreaming. I was really following a damn cat out of this warehouse to safety. The quiet chuckle breached my lips as I thought about it, and I couldn't help but to shake my head.

"What now? All of the guards are outside, and I am not in the best shape to do much of anything, especially running. Or shit, fighting either with one eye."

As if it was communicating with something, the cat stood still and stared at the ground. Suddenly, I noticed the guards were moving toward the front of the building in the direction of the woods. Another unnaturally large, breathtaking cat strolled up. This one had bright silvery eyes that was a considerable contrast to the coal black fur. As if this was normal, it kneeled as to tell me to climb on. With a little nudge from the first cat, I was able to get up without much grunting.

We took off toward the back of the warehouse into the woods in the opposite direction of all of the commotion. I turned to look back and saw a pretty brown-skinned woman I didn't see her inside the entire time I was there, but she reminded me of Jamilah. Couldn't be? A question clawed at me; why did she just let us go? She could have alerted Shadow and caught us in action.

Gripping the soft fur, I held on for dear life as I trusted these big ass cats to take me to safety. It wasn't like I had many other options. Stay and continue to get my ass handed to me by the security gorillas, or take a chance and trust two random cats that I might know, but not really.

With explosive grace, the big cats surged into the moonlight, swallowed by the woods. My big cat brought up the rear, being guided with swift prowess. The smooth ride lulled my weak body into darkness.

"I don't know anything!" I yelled out as my body jolted awake. Body drenched in a cold sweat, I sat up in a bed unfamiliar to me at first sight. The earthy-sweet smell of chamomile wafted through my senses. "What time is it?"

The sun wasn't out, so maybe it was nighttime. The only light in the room was from the moon shining bright into the bedroom window. Looking over at the nightstand, the phone charger clock showed 10:15pm. I pulled back the silky soft cream covers, then realized I was half naked. Somebody must have bathed me and put my pajama pants on my body. I knew it was Nia, or at least I hoped it was. Thinking of my baby and how she had taken care of me had me smiling hard. I winced at the pain in my face. How soon I forgot about the beatdown from them silver back gorillas.

I trusted you, and you lied to me. You are just like all of the other lying, cheating ass men in this world.

Damn, this girl must have had the volume of this TV on 100. Here she went watching her reality TV. I noticed Reality TV, or as I liked to call it, ratchet TV, was her guilty pleasure. When she was stressed, Reality Tv. When she was unwinding from the day, Reality TV. Bored, Reality TV. This was definitely her go to for relaxation. Now that I was back, I wondered if that was what was bothering her? Did they uncover anything new?

"Hey baby!" ,came out hoarser than intended. I guess my recovery would take a little longer than expected. Her head snapped in my direction, and Nia jumped when she saw me standing at the bottom of the stairs leading into the bedroom. "I guess you didn't hear me walking in because you were fully immersed in your ratchet TV," I said as I slowly sat next to her on the couch. After what I had been through, this couch felt like clouds straight from heaven.

She sat on the couch in her favorite position, her legs criss-crossed underneath her body, with a glass of wine on the coffee table and a bowl full of popcorn. She was fully engaged in her favorite reality tv show, Real Working Women of Miramar. It looked like someone's man was keeping secrets again, and the shit blew up in his face at a restaurant.

"What did Braxton do this time?"

"Look at you knowing somebody's name. I thought you hated these shows."

Nia smirked and patted the seat on the couch beside her.

"I do, you just keep them playing all day and night. It didn't take long for me to catch on."

"Well, Braxton was withholding info from Dawn, and of course, it came out at the worst time."

I slowly sat next to Nia on the couch listening to her explain what was happening. My body was a little stiff and still sore, but another hot bath with epsom salt would help. As I adjusted myself on the couch, I noticed her movements become rigid as she continued to explain. Tilting my head to the side, I quirked my eyebrow up looking in her direction. Guilt.

"I know we haven't known each other for very long, but I told you I could read you like a book. Plus, reading people was my actual job in the military. What is going on with you? Don't bull shit me either. I know you are withholding something. Is it about my dad?"

With a deep inhale, then an even longer exhale, Nia sat up then turned her body toward me on the plush couch. She fidgeted with her fingers. "Wait a minute."

She grabbed her phone to turn the living room light on bright to help with changing the vibe in the room. Gone was the cute, cozy vibe, and in its place was a rigid, sterile like scene. This conversation had to be serious since she needed to see my reaction when she told me her secret.

"How are you feeling after being kidnapped and tortured? Do you want to talk about it?" She was slowly gauging my mood before whatever news she had, before she dropped it in my lap.

"Well, I didn't know what to expect at first. I had to lean heavily on my military background to get through it. Two big gorilla looking dudes kicked my ass to get me to talk about my dad but I had nothing to give them. I truly have no info."

I shrugged my shoulders then winced at the shooting pain in my body from the small movement. My ribs throbbed every time I made any major moves. "I may have brain damage from the beatings because I know I started hallucinating. Two big ass cats came to my rescue, and I rode on one of their backs until I fell asleep then woke up here. The craziest part of it all is one of those big ass cats felt so familiar."

I knew I sounded crazy. The blank stare she had on her face didn't give me much to go on.

"About that..." She blew out a deep breathe. "I have a major secret. I am not sure how to tell you."

She held this weird smile on her face, but her eyebrows bunched in the middle. Thinking back on my military training, some people struggled with exposing themselves. They tended to laugh or smile during awkward or intense situations that were hard to handle. Their faces could show a variety of expressions. This must be something big.

Biting her lip to keep the smile from expanding, she took a deep breath... "I have wrestled with sharing this with you, since we decided to get closer. My family and I are all panther shifters. I mean, everyone but Jamilah. We don't know what's going..."

"Wait!" I interjected before she continued to ramble.

She closed her eyes and held her breath waiting to see how I would respond. The tension was so thick in the air, you could cut it with a butter knife. I knew Nia's mind was going a million miles a minute now.

Would I switch up like the rest of the guys?

That was her biggest complaint when we discussed her previous relationships. It all made so much sense now. But...damn!

"H-How is that even possible? Your dad too?"

I stood up and started to pace the living room floor. I had heard of this type of thing before, but I thought it was all just a myth.

"Yes, even my dad," she said timidly. I could tell she was slowly retreating back in her head. I needed her to know different.

Walking back to the couch, I sat beside her. "This doesn't change how I feel, but I have to admit, I don't know much about this stuff. You would have to teach me everything. Your heart is pure, and that's what I care about the most."

She sat there in silence, scouring my face to see if there were any signs of deception. Her eyes began to water, and I couldn't have my baby crying. Everything was coming together now.

"I knew those eyes looked familiar. It was you? The big ass cat that came in the room to get me, right?"

"Panthers! Not big cats, but yes. It was me. Are you OK with that?"

"So, who was the other ca- I mean... panther? Was that your dad?" She nodded silently. "He is humongous!"

Nia chuckled and exhaled hard, melting into the couch like she'd just unloaded a truth too heavy to carry.

Jumping to my feet, I remembered. "Wait! Who was that in the forest behind your house? I had a whole conversation with what I think was a panther."

She slightly bowed her head; her actions confirmed my suspicions that it was indeed Nia in the forest that day.

Chapter 14

Jamilah

A loud, thunderous boom blared out in the air. Feet shuffled quickly outside of the doorway. Several armed men headed to one direction, weapons drawn ready to engage. My head whipped in several directions in search of the issue behind the commotion. I ran down the hall to the security room. What could have caused such a disruption at the warehouse tonight? It backed up to a forest and was pretty desolate in the area. Unless it was wildlife, who would be in this area unless they knew what was out here?

I came here to see if I could gather an update on Jerome Carter. In turn, I think I had walked into a possible ambush. Seeing that the issue was just possible wildlife, I could move on to find Shadow. Maybe Shadow had some new intel for me. Jerome was being hidden and well-protected. I needed a new angle, and I guess I was still trying to work through killing my sister's in-law. This was going to cause all kinds of tension and possibly ruin the little relationship that we actually had with each other. Forget any hopes of us getting closer after this was done.

Shaking out of those thoughts, I needed to get to Shadow so I could get out of here. It is what it is in this situation. She might forgive me, eventually. Especially once I told her everything. The gray, empty halls magnified the clacking of my stiletto heels on the concrete floor. This visit felt off. Eery. The chill in the air was unlike an air conditioner cooling the room. This was a bone chilling cold. The powerful stench of copper caused me to scrunch my face, as the smell assaulted my nose. Blood. What the hell was going on here?

Throughout the warehouse, a strong, putrid, coppery scent was heavy in the air. A trail of dried blood led from the far wall to the interrogation room. Stopping at the dimly lit interrogation room littered with blood sprayed on the walls, I peaked through the glass on the door.

"Oh, snap! Is that Xavier?" I whispered to myself.

Stepping back from the door, I covered my mouth with my hand. I had no clue they had grabbed Jerome's son. They must have taken him from his home when Nia wasn't around. Shit! That only meant Nia would be coming for him shortly.

If I knew my sister like I thought I did, this as all bad. Once she made it here, things would escalate and quickly. I needed to be far away from here by the time she arrived. I was not about to get my ass handed to me by an angry panther. Growing up, I was never able to best her. Not even in a sneak attack. Her panther was top tier prowler and hunter. I could not get anything past her.

Xavier looked pretty badly beaten when I walked in to scope the scene. Things must have gotten crazy during the interrogation. "Aw, hell no!"

She hadn't had a man in a long time, and now when she got one, he got kidnapped and beaten. Jumping up and down, I spun around looking to get the hell out of here. She was going to tear this place apart.

"Who is going to be here when she gets here? Not I, said the cat."

Turning on my heels to head back to my car, an eerie quiet came over the cold empty warehouse. I knew that meant something was happening. This silence was too quiet, exposing, spine chilling. The slow creek from the back door caused me to stand stark still in a dark cove. My breath hitched when I saw the large panther prowl down the hall like a predator looking for its prey. I knew she would come for him. Things seemed to be going good with her and Xavier, so it was only right. I wondered who else was in on this. She didn't make an announcement to the group text to inform anyone that he was missing, unless she kept me out of the loop, as usual. A lump formed in my throat at the thought, and I rolled my eyes.

The panther stopped at the door, gazing at the wall with the trail of blood. Just as I thought, the golden eyed panther—Nia.

I would recognize that glare anywhere. She was all grace and vengeance. Stealth and danger. She stalked straight into the room he was held in, then led her battered boyfriend to the door. As they walked toward the still forest, they were joined by another larger panther. This one was much larger and coat blacker than night, my dad. I knew this was a family affair, but how much did they know? Standing in the doorway, I locked eyes with Xavier, but he didn't alert them I was watching. Hell, he probably didn't recognize me with only one eye. The other was swollen shut.

I stood in the threshold of the exit and just stared in amazement. The majestic beasts sauntered off into the greenery of the woods. Grumbling to myself, I said, "If only I was able to shift, maybe they would accept me as one of them."

A weight appeared on my chest I never felt before. The black sheep of the family. Hell, if I could shift into a sheep, that would be better than not being able to shift at all. Just a regular human that they called when they needed something.

Why am I so different? What is wrong with me?

The burden of being the only Grant to not be able to shift kept me feeling alone in this shifter world. I was just the computer girl with the shifter name but no shifter power to back it up.

I needed to figure out my path, maybe get away from the Onyx Hunt. I hadn't committed to this new organization with Shadow. After tonight, I wasn't so sure I wanted to. Watching

Dad and Nia disappear into the trees brought back my feelings of yearning... acheing... longing. Taking Shadow's offer meant I could still do this, but on my own terms. It wouldn't hurt to explore my options. I still had too much to think about.

The warehouse faded behind me, but the ache in my chest didn't. If I was ever going to understand what was broken in me, I needed answers. I knew of a place that held that kind of truth. Calling my sister, Aaliyah, I asked her to keep the library open a little late for me.

I needed to get into Blackwater's Historical Library to see if I could find something on shifting later in life than at puberty, as expected. With Blackwater being a "hidden shifter town" there was much knowledge of the shifter realm here. They had a special collections section that might be able to lend me some assistance. It was kept locked up and heavily guarded for its secrets. Most humans could not handle the truth found in these historical documents, and the government couldn't be trusted to have in-depth knowledge of it either. Before I made a grave mistake and committed to the wrong organization, I needed to know if there was any chance I would still shift. Even outside of the normal timeframe.

"I don't plan to be there long, maybe thirty minutes. I do not want to run into Genesis' crazy ass. She freaks me out. She has this big hair and pretty face but is a stone-cold killer. Literally."

Shivers ran through my body as I thought of the many stories from Aaliyah. We laughed loudly at our brief time catching up then hung up. I was probably closer to her, out of all my sisters. I needed to let her know I didn't have time for any miscommunications with that damn gargoyle or her family.

After leaving the library, I was more confused than when I started. According to my research, there were not many reasons for me to not shift. Heavy trauma during the shifting period or puberty or DNA factors. Whatever that meant. My mom and dad had three other healthy shifters, but when it was my turn, something was wrong. They were old, sure, but panthers were normally not affected like regular humans with medical issues.

Maybe I just needed more patience. The only issue there was, it didn't help with the major decision I had on the table. Shadow wanted me to come join his company to be a part of the hunters, but I wanted to be with family. My heart was with the Onyx Hunt. That company raised me and taught me everything I knew about the business. I couldn't turn my back on it. Even if they turned their back on me.

"Ugh!" I screamed, frustrated, as I pulled my car away from the library parking lot.

Slowly, I pulled into Lucky's Wingspot for a late night snack and a drink. Being an emotional eater, this was my spot for good food and drinks when I had a lot on my mind. My heart smiled as I walked in to find my spot at the bar open. This corner seat let me see the whole place, and I had a great view of Mr. Sexy right next to it. Hopping on the barstool, I decided to flirt a little. "Just in time for the last game. Who you rooting for tonight?"

He was bringing his beer to his lips as I asked my question but stopped as it touched his lips. Looking over in my direction, he never put the beer down when he said, "I'm here to watch the game, not mingle." He turned his head back toward the TV and continued to drink his beer.

Oh, snap! He was too sexy to be such an asshole. Sucks too, since I was looking for some entertainment tonight. He thoroughly ignored my presence the entire game. He was friendly with the bartender which only led me to believe he just didn't like my ass. I shrugged my shoulders as I thought about it. Oh, well! He wouldn't be the first asshole to not know greatness when they saw it. Eating my wings and downing beers made up for the sour mood I was in before I came tonight.

"Aight, Malik. See ya later, dude!" the bartender yelled out as the asshat next to me stood to leave. I couldn't lie, he was fine as hell. Big, burly chocolate man. He was tatted up, but his waves could make a girl seasick. A little rough around the edges, but I ain't never scared. I shook my head as I thought about all of that goodness going to waste.

"You shouldn't stay out too late by yourself. It's some crazy people out here looking to start up conversations with strangers," he said to me as I looked up into his dark gaze. I could have sworn I saw a shimmer in his eyes... signs of a shifter. The eyeroll that came next was so hard, I made myself dizzy.

Why do I always run across assholes?

"Boy, fuck you!" He wasn't just a regular asshole; he had to be a shifter on top of it. That was ten times worse. They all had an air about them.

He chuckled, pulled his hoodie over his head, and walked off. His big, linebacker ass even looked good from behind. Glad I dodged that bullet. Watching my sisters date shifters, let me know I needed to steer clear of those problems. Gathering my things, I tipped the bartender then headed home for some rest before I was back on the hunt for Jerome.

Chapter 15

Timothy

I am getting too old for this shit, I thought, shifting back from our little rescue adventure in the woods.

A quiet home awaited me when I walked in, Shirley sound asleep. The lamp on my side table was the only light for my large study room. Historical books lined the walls and casted a shadow on my desk. As I walked into my office, my mind shuffled through different thoughts about our most bizarre case this year. There were several red flags about all of this, and I had to get answers TONIGHT. I needed to start by researching that warehouse. Who was it registered to? Burning the midnight oil was on the agenda tonight so we could move past this. We had been going in circles for far too long with no answers.

Thinking back on tonight's events, I scented Jamilah for some odd reason. I didn't get a chance to bring it up with Nia, with the state we found Xavier in, but I know for sure I scented my child. My youngest baby had always had a hard time accepting not being able to shift. She felt left out of the biggest inside secret of Florida. It oftentimes caused her to act out when she was in her feelings. Was she out following us? That would be a new one. That couldn't be it, her scent was strongest between the warehouse doors. She had to be inside or was inside at one time. That was weird. I couldn't even get her to run the surveillance cameras in the area because then she would know we knew about her following us.

But the question was why would she be there or following us unless she was tied to Jerome in some way? That didn't make any sense. How could they be connected? Rubbing my forehead, I had to press on to find something. Anything.

Moving on to look up my best friend, I ran across some interesting things. He was still stepping out on his wife. These bank statements from an account he thought he could hide showed his many rendezvous'. Could this be a woman scorned? Maybe one of his prospects that hoped for more. Biting my pen, I crossed my arms over my chest and leaned back in my chair. "That means I need to go back and create a list. All of the women he has ever slept with. This damn list will be as long as a CVS receipt."

I buried my face in my hands, surrendering to the truth—finding sleep would be a battle I'd lose tonight.

A total of twenty-five women in the thirty-seven years he had been married. Damn! What was the point of getting married?

"Dude has been busy. Let's see who are all of these woman."

After a few clicks on my computer keyboard, I had a few names and a few locations. One location in particular stood out. That was Shirley's favorite spot when her and her friends wanted to get away. She had never invited me or planned a couples vacation for us there, so I had no clue what was there to do. It must be a great tourist spot, since they had been going there for over twenty years. I wondered had they ever run into each other. She never mentioned it. She didn't really speak on her vacations at all now that I thought of it.

A few more hours on the computer, and some shit started looking really crazy. Either I was delirious from the lack of sleep, or somebody was going to be in danger very soon. Shirley and Jerome seemed to frequent a lot of some of the same places. Mind racing and feet pacing, back and forth in my office, I stared out of the window. This motherfucker cheated with *my* wife? My body stilled, and I felt as if the air had been sucked out of the room. With my chest heavy and my anger rising, I was holding on by a thread.

The sun was now shining bright into my office, my eyes dry from glaring at my computer for hours. The night long gone and sleep evaded. Icy, hot tingles beneath my skin around my neck caused sweat to form on my forehead. I needed air.

"I need to go for a run," came out as a gravely growl as I sped past Shirley sitting in the living room watching TV. She sat straight up in her seat looking bewildered with her mouth opened as my body virtually vibrated at the door. My heart beat slowed in agony as I looked into her eyes. I turned to the door, and with my forehead on the glass, huffed out an exaggerated exhale.

Stepping outside, I leapt from the back porch and transformed midair in to my panther. The serene greenery of the forest dulled the raging storm in my mind to a quiet hum. The stabbing pain in my chest temporarily subsided with every beat of my panther's paws pounding the ground. Dust wafted in the air from my speed and agility as I moved across decaying leaves, stirring up the strong smell of jasmine in the air.

It'd been way too long since I had been able to release stress from a run, to escape, and to outrun the ache of betrayal burning in my gut. My wife and my best friend. Running from the house as fast as I could to avoid destroying my house and my marriage, I jumped in a tree, climbed to the top, and hung from the branch until it came crashing down. The throbbing ache from my head hitting the ground did not do enough to distract me from the stabbing pain in my chest. When I stood to my feet, I rushed to the nearest bush and gripped it with my teeth to yank it from the depths of the earth. Extended claws and stamina kept me busy swiping at the medium sized trees until a small area was totally cleared. Finally exhausting myself with the destruction, I noticed the bitter taste of bile slowly decreasing. The rage subsiding and now questions and more questions.

The burn of my muscles cried out for a break as I neared the clear, quiet creek. My panther's connection to the forest went beyond the spiritual—it was healing even during my rage, grief, and...hurt. What did this newfound information mean for my marriage, my friendship...my kids? Staring into the creek for answers, a thought crossed my mind as my eyes glistened with unshed tears.

Are the girls even mine?

I grabbed my clothes stash and decided to take a walk into town, I left the peace and comfort of the forest. I couldn't hide there forever. Headed to grab a bite to eat at Lucky's Wingspot, I planned to get a few beers then head back to the house for this inevitable conversation. I was going to get to the bottom of all this betrayal, then I could decide how to move forward. Not until I disassociated for a while and lived in the numbness with my football and beers.

Crossing the busy street, I noticed Jamilah standing in a parking lot talking to a tall, menacing man I had never seen before. With the body language and animation from her, I would assume it to be a heated conversation. Making my presence known was a must, just in case I needed to break his face.

"Hey, baby girl!" I said, noticing her body stiffen at the sound of my voice.

"H-heyy, Daddy," she said hesitantly. Something was off with her. With them. What the hell was going with my baby girl? She should know not to keep anything from me.

Reaching my hand out, I introduced myself to the man she was previously speaking with, I said, "Hi, I am Jamilah's Dad, Timothy. Are you her boyfriend?"

My eyes roved over the young man from head to toe. He was dressed neatly in black slacks and a white dress shirt with French cuff sleeves. His cuff links were a modest matte black with the letter L on top. The L blended into the black, barely noticeable. His look screamed powerful businessman. What did Jamilah get herself tied into now?

Reaching his large, tattooed hand out and strongly embracing my hand, he straightened his back, squared his shoulders and looked me straight in the eye. His gaze intense as if he tried to stare into my soul. Gripping my hand, he stated, "I have heard so much about you, Mr. Timothy. My name is Shadow. Former military as well and not Jamilah's boyfriend. I am more of a... business associate."

"Nice to meet you, Shadow. I was just heading into Lucky's for wings and beer. You guys are welcome to join me."

"Hey, y'all. What are you all doing here?" We all turned to see another one of my daughters, Keisha, standing with a friend. Six curious eyes stared at the newcomers as they waited to be introduced to the new guy, Shadow.

Watching Shadow, he looked like a star struck celebrity fan looking at Keisha. This big scary looking man couldn't formulate a sentence when she walked up. So, he definitely wasn't

Jamilah's boyfriend. He might be trying to push up on Keisha if he could.

"Hey, baby girl! What are y'all doing out here?" I said, trying to break up the tension building between Shadow and Keisha. Reaching out I grabbed her pulling her in for a hug.

"We just wanted to come and get some beer and wings. You know Lucky's has the best in town."

Keisha stood with her arm looped through her friend's arm. She giggled out looking up shyly at Shadow. I had never seen my always serious detective daughter so girly and giddy. This was a welcomed change for my inquisitive and always serious daughter. I don't know if I like the idea of Shadow being the one to bring it out of her though. She needed some romantic love and affection in her life. She couldn't just cling to family and work and have a healthy balance at life.

"Well, ladies!" he said to all the women, but his eyes were focused on Keisha. "Enjoy your lunch, it's time for me to head out and take care of some business."

He turned his body to address me, then said, "It was nice to meet you, Mr. Timothy." He then walked to stand in front of Keisha, his large frame shaded her from the sun, he said, "Maybe next time we meet, I can show you a real wing place that will beat Lucky's, hands down."

He reached his large hand out to take hers in his hand then brought it to his lips. Confidently, he strutted to his white Mercedes S550 AMG with white rims and mirror tint. My eyebrows shot up at the gesture.

I need to vet this young whippersnapper before she becomes too involved with him, I thought. He seemed like the type of man to go after what he wanted and didn't hear the word *no* often.

Her and her friend walked into Lucky's as I stood out with Jamilah watching. Jamilah's body language was still rigid, but she seemed to be a little relieved that Shadow was gone. I hoped she didn't get herself into any trouble the Onyx would have to bail her out of soon. She was a good kid, but her bitterness from not being able to shift oftentimes overshadowed it. She would act out or isolate herself from us because she felt left out. We didn't want to exclude her in our activities, but sometimes, she just couldn't participate. Hopefully, her shift happened soon. I saw her slowly spiraling because of it, and I couldn't save her from everything.

Chapter 16

Shadow

Standing in a dark corner of the parking lot, I watched people pass by carry on with life, completely oblivious to their surroundings. No one had a clue someone was watching. People were so careless with their situational awareness. Jamilah pulled her car in to a parking spot and just sat. She sat there with a heavy look on her face. A look of worry and despair. What had she uncovered that would solicit this feeling? Of course, she didn't see me as I stood in the shadows and just observed. Her hands gripped the steering wheel tight, and her eyes focused on nothing in particular. She was cracking. Not broken. Yet. But close. Something had changed. Her mind wavering. I need answers on what was going on.

At the top of my list of questions, why was Jerome still alive? She only had one assignment. With her family connections, she should have been able to get in when no one else could. I did not want to take matters into my own hands and started snapping necks, but if I had to, I would with no hesitation. I needed this shit taken care of expeditiously. And I needed it to be brutal.

Walking up and using my knuckles, I tapped on her window in three wraps. There was a slight jump then pause. She took a deep breath before she got out the car. Jamilah was clearly off her game. Me walking up to her should have never been a surprise. If she wanted the respect she always stated she deserved, she had to come harder than this. Hesitation marred her features, as if she was nervous about something.

Standing out in front of a few businesses, I knew we couldn't dive deep into too much, but I needed something. She chose this place, maybe for witnesses. I admit, I had been on edge about all of this, but when a job needed to be done, I expected results. This had gone on far longer than I normally allowed. With my arms folded behind my back, I started, "Hi, Ms. Grant! Give me an update on your assignment."

Straight to the point. My tone was even, and my body posture was non-threatening. I needed her to feel at ease speaking with me for several reasons.

"It's been weeks, and this mission is not complete. I had full trust that you could handle this. Was I mistaken?"

Tilting my head to the side, I stopped talking to allow her the space to begin. I was not only listening to her words but watching her actions. I needed to know her motivations and read her soul.

"No, I can handle my mission. Its just that in light of some new information I received, things have been delayed. I have been watching my dad and his computer activity through my SpyWare software."

As she talked, I was taken aback at her words. "I have found some new information that I think we should take into consideration for this mission."

I listened to what she had to say, but I wasn't impressed. Instead of watching her father, she should have been watching the target. Jerome was still affiliated with sex traffickers, and he had to die. She obviously thought I wanted her opinion on the targets that I assigned. Folding my left arm and rubbing my beard with my right hand, I had many questions. "So, let me get this straight. You're stalling because your spyware caught your daddy watching porn?" I said sarcastically.

"No. I'm stalling because I found documents that may include larger players in this. If your goal is to take down everyone involved, we don't want to start taking out all the low level minions and spook the big fish in this game."

I stroked my beard as I listened. She actually had a point.

"They will stop all trafficking and change their plans. You will be back at square one."

Fuck! Wiping my hand down my face, I took a deep breath. She was right. Don't want to alert the bigger players. I stared deep into her eyes as to read any hint of deception. I would end all this right now and do it myself if I felt she was lying to me.

There was nervousness but no deception. She knew something, but I guess I had to wait to find out what.

Taking a step forward, I lowered my voice when I looked right into her eyes. "I don't give second chances when it comes to missions not being executed. I trust you. For now. I will allow you to continue to research. But as soon as you find some—"

A determined stranger approached. Taking a small step back, I cut off my statement. This conversation didn't need any extra eats. He looked mighty comfortable with her. Her father. This was great. The target's best friend. I wonder if he knew his best friend had fucked his wife and liked to help with the kidnapping of children.

As he introduced himself, I got the vibe that he was a decent dude being nosey because his daughter was talking to a strange man. I made sure to stand up straighter to give the appearance of a good guy, not a threat. He was dressed in simple running gear, sweatpants and a t-shirt. I saw him checking me out trying to read me. Typical. His file said he was a military man and I wouldn't expect anything less. I knew how to charm a Parent and thankfully I had read his file thoroughly. I held a quick conversation about nothing with an over-protective father, we were pleasantly interrupted by two fine, chocolate ladies that looked related to the Grants in some way.

This woman was even more beautiful in person. I remembered her face from Jamilah's profile. She must be Keisha, the detective. Big hair and an even bigger personality. I was stuck.

Her lips called to me and, watching her, so did her eyes. She stood and stared into my soul. Bold. Beautiful. She didn't flinch when I returned her intensity. Most grown men would falter but not Keisha. I was truly intrigued.

Watching her mannerisms, she was softer than her file suggested. Her body faced me, not her sister, not her dad. It was subtle, but I caught it. An unspoken invitation just for me. A quiet opening to engage her. I loved that I could bring that out of her, but we could never be. I'm the bad boy that ladies loved to fawn over. There was no future in that though. I was flattered that my presence made her giddy, but until business was finished, pleasure would have to wait.

The mission remained the same—kill those affiliated with child trafficking. The Onyx Hunt might have kept Keisha out of the loop about the current chaos surrounding Jerome. But I knew once we killed him, things would change with my chances of getting to know her on an intimate level. It was best to not engage in anything past flirting. No info exchanging.

This situation deserved my loyalty and dedication far more than I deserved the right to lust after a female I barely knew. I needed heads to roll. Bodies to drop. The right people to come up missing. *I remember the scream. The silence. The void. The pain. The toys still in the front yard, abandoned. I still smell the burnt rubber from tires of the vehicle that took her.*

She was taken from a life where she was loved, protected, and cared for and sold i to only God knows what. I thought about her daily—her struggles, her fears, her torture. I clenched my jaw as my thoughts ran rampant and headed to my car to get back to my office. That pain hit my chest and knocked my ass right back into reality.

Since the kidnapping, I had worked my ass off to be in the best possible situation to dismantle the organization that was in charge of the trafficking ring. I went into the military, endured the madness of deployment multiple times, got the best possible training I could for mental and physical warfare. My life haf been dedicated to learning The Who and infiltrating whatever organization I needed to in order to take them down. So far, we had found out about senators, doctors, nurses and even some judges that were in at the inception of the ring.

I pulled into my parking spot at the office and took out my cell phone. "Since Jamilah is having second thoughts about helping, I'll just force her hand."

The ringing phone was answered on the third ring, though it rang for what felt like forever.

I breathlessly answered, "Hello! This is Nia."

Chapter 17

Jamilah

Sitting in my office, the room dark and quiet, my mind raced. I had just pulled my blackout curtains to conceal the room from any form of outside light and distraction. My computer screen casted a faint blue haze over the wall, the only artificial light in the room. The only sound competing with my thoughts was the quiet hum of the AC. My chest tightened with every second that passed.

"I need a drink to deal with this shit."

I got up, walked to my small bar in the corner of my office. Not being a heavy drinker, my options were very limited. Settling on my favorite dark liquor, Crown Royal Apple flavor with two cubes of ice. I fumbled with the tongs for the ice until finally I dug my hands in the ice maker to get what I needed. My hands shook as I poured it in my glass. Slowly sipping, I continued to wrap my mind around this new piece of info I just found out. The slight burn in my chest distracted me from the storm in my head. A calm washed over my senses as the liquor flowed through my system. The info I read from my dad's computer was on a continuous loop in my mind. I felt the heaviness this new info carried in the pit of my stomach. Our lives had changed forever.

My mom and my dad's best-friend were having an affair. When did she have time...those girls trips? I remembered her coming back more calm and relaxed. I guess it was more than the beach to have that affect on her. Why, though? A scowl crept across my face as I thought about the betrayal. To my daddy. To my family. Daddy did everything for her. We never needed anything, and he always supported her in her hobbies and activities. No matter how crazy or taxing they were on all of us.

Rocking back and forth in my office chair, I allowed my thoughts to wander until it hit me. My breath hitched.

"Could he be any of our dads? Oh, shit! Is he my dad?"

Turning to walk toward the window, I leaned my body against the wall, pulled my curtains back, and stared into the sky, eyes filled with unshed tears. "That would make so much sense. I am the only one who can't shift. Everybody else is full panther."

Whispering when realization hit me, I covered my mouth, "Maybe he is my dad, and that is why I can't shift because I am only half panther. I need to go talk to my mom."

My lips trembled at the overwhelming feeling of sadness. In a bout of anger, the short glass in my hand flew against the wall and shattered, wasting all of my good liquor. I screamed, "SHIT!"

When I was finally able to gather myself, I dressed grabbed my keys and headed out the door. Pushing my Benz to the limit, I weaved in and out of traffic to get to my parents house to get some answers. My heart raced and so did my mind. The feeling of betrayal laid heavy on my chest. Did my dad know about all of this? He was going to be crushed when he found out if he didn't already know. I knew all of the info came from his computer, but did he connect the dots, or was he going to ignore the signs? This new information changed everything for everyone.

Slowly, I gathered myself and walked to the door. I wasn't ready. Taking a deep breath, I moved in closer and heard loud arguing. Dad definitely knew, and he had chosen to face it head on. "How long, Shirley? How long did you *play in my face* as the kids say? I gave you everything you could have ever wanted or needed, and this is what you do?"

I heard his pained voice belt out those words as I walked around the corner in to the living area. He was standing in the kitchen behind the island to keep his body held back from tearing her head off. Mom stood in the open living room looking horrified. All confidence and poise stripped away by my dad's anger at this situation.

The air in the room was so thick you could cut the tension with a butter knife. The once lively and colorful vibe the decor of the living room brought felt dark and shaded under the news of infidelity looming high off the ceiling. Two sets of bloodshot eyes looked over to me with pain, hurt and...guilt lining their emotions. Why did Daddy feel guilt?

My dad walked over to me, greeting and hugging me. "Hey, baby girl!" He tried to mask his pain with his forced cheerfulness. I felt his pain and anguish as he winced at the sound of his own voice. He was cracking. She had broken him.

I started, "Let's not play pretend. I know. I saw everything on Dad's computer."

Their bodies stiffened under my words, but at this time, I only cared about getting answers. Looking both of my parents in the eyes, I saw my dad had many questions for me, but I knew he would wait. My mom looked like a frightened child caught with her hand in the cookie jar.

"Is it true, Mom?" I said with a firm tone and sheer determination in my eyes to obtain the truth.

"What are you talking about, little girl? Whatever you *think* you know is between my husband and I," she said with her nose pushed in the air.

"And what do you have on?" A small gasp left my mouth. Shirley Grant actually had the nerve to say that to me in the midst of this situation. I guess she would do or say anything to deflect from her shortcomings.

Ignoring her attempt at changing the subject, I walked further into the living room. "Well, that was exactly why I came by. I wanted to look you in your face to ask you, is Jerome Carter my dad?"

The silence in the room was loud and anxiety-filled. My dad looked devastated as his head swiveled back and forth from my face then back to my mom. After a moment of silence, I screamed, "You knew?"

With my face scrunched up into a ball, my eyebrows touched my hairline. "Ugh!" My lip curled, my body cringed as I turned to walk away.

Pacing back and forth in the living room, my head down, I hugged my body for comfort. My dad was radiating anger, and the feral look in his eyes caused an uneasy feeling in my gut. He was on the brink of shifting to his Panther when I walked over to embrace him in a hug. The dam broke at our embrace. He wrapped his arms around my body, and for the first time in a long time, I felt safe, seen, and... loved. His body wrapped around my tiny frame, and I could tell this was needed for us both. He loved me and my sisters, and to know that my mother robbed me of having this man as my father broke something inside of me. Nausea filled my stomach as the world around me spun. He held me tight until my sobs quieted.

"Baby girl... in spite of this new information, I still love you. We will always be family."

His eyes glistened as he looked into my soul and proclaimed his love for his family. Even in the midst of his own pain, he took the time to make sure I was OK. Shirley Grant had single-handedly destroyed half of her family with her selfish ways. I didn't know how we would recover from this new discovery.

Before Daddy released his hold on me, he leaned into my ear, and the air around the room shifted. He was, in that moment, in work mode by the look in his eyes. His voice low and steady, brought goosebumps to my neck. "I have a few questions for you. Come to The Onyx this afternoon so we can talk. I love you!"

He walked out of the living room toward the backdoor. When he stepped outside and closed the door, he took in the fresh air then shifted to his panther. His large panther with the shiny coat had always been a sight to see. I studied my dad appreciatively as he ran toward the lush greenery that was the forest. This resilient and complex man who always stayed ahead of the game was brought to his knees by the people closest to him. Even if he was not my father, that man still had my heart.

Chapter 18

Nia

"Meet me at the Onyx now," my dad roared through the phone as soon as I answered. His tone was certain and serious. This could only mean he had some new information to share. This could be really good or really bad. I guess we would find out shortly.

"Hello to you, too, Daddy! Xavier and I will be there."

Chuckling a little at how straightforward my dad was, I moved to Xavier sitting on the back porch. He had been a little withdrawn since experiencing and surviving the abduction. Instead of walking out and updating him on the latest request, I stood at the glass door and took him all in. His body was built tough, but his heart and mind were weary.

Since being back in Blackwater Bay he had had a lot thrown at him. Recovering from the crazy breakup, his family being in danger, taken hostage, and the latest—unveiling my family secret. That wasn't even the end. His family was still in danger.

Something was going on with his dad, and my gut feeling was telling me it was big. I didn't want to add more to his plate than what he could handle. He sat and watched the forest.

Sliding the glass door open, the noise from the rollers caught Xavier's attention. The slacked disillusionment on his face and rapid blinking caused my heart to hurt when he tried to mask it. I felt his overwhelm. Walking to him, I sat on his lap, getting lost in his eyes. I inquired about his mental health in an around about way. "What's on your mind, babe?"

"I'm good. Just relaxing out in nature," he responded without actually engaging with me.

I tore the band-aid off and let him know, "We have been summoned to the Onyx. Daddy has some info he needs to share with us."

I stood up, grabbed his hand, and led him into the bedroom. Before he could put his clothes on, I walked to him and looked up to him in his eyes and placed a soft kiss on his lips. Wrapping my arms around his neck, I stood on my tip toes to reach comfortably. He needed what I had to offer, and I was willing to give it to him.

I wanted to be his resting place and solace when the world got too loud. He helped me grow in accepting who I am, so I would be there to hold my gentle giant up when needed. Rubbing my hands down his chest, past his ripped abs and over his denim pants, I kissed him softly and reached in his jeans to grab his bulging member.

His breath hitched as my fingers struggled to wrap around him. Pulling his jeans and boxers to the ground, I pushed him backward until he was stopped by the bed. Falling back onto the bed, he allowed me to take the lead in his pleasure. After removing his pants and underwear, I reached for the hem of his t-shirt to pull over his head. His arms went above his head, and I locked his arms with his shirt there. I kept them there while I kissed down his muscular chest and enjoyed every second of him unravel beneath my touch. Brushing my lips over the light display of hair from his belly button to his pelvis area, I was enjoying this more than him. Grabbing his shaft, I stretched my tongue out to taste the pre-cum beaded at the tip. My eyes rolled to the back of my head with pleasure as my tastebuds exploded with ecstasy.

Xavier hummed in pleasure as I worked him over with my mouth. Before he could explode in my mouth, I climbed up his body and let him know I wanted all of what he had to offer inside of me. I continued to hold his arms locked in place above his head while I sat on his large veiny dick and worked him over. The sounds coming from Xavier was all the motivation I needed to "Finish Him..." in my Mortal Combat voice.

His legs trembled under me. To increase the euphoria, I held the control. I kissed him passionately, overloading his body with feelings of pleasure leaving no room for thoughts of worry. At the feel of his balls draw tight, I whispered in his ear, "I love you!"

His warm spirts of cum shot off inside of me. His eyes, once shut tight, flew open in surprise and softened as I repeated the declaration. We both laid in bed skin to skin, unmoved, basking in our climax as we waited for our breathing to regulate. We needed to get up. My dads waiting at the Onyx.

The drive over to the Onyx was quiet as Xavier sped through the city, mind on finally getting answers. His body was still bruised, but he was working through healing daily. He refused to allow me to help him as if I were trying to coddle him. My mind was stuck on the call I received earlier from a Shadow. He was very mysterious and didn't answer any of my questions. He just kept asking if I really knew my boyfriend's family. He told me to look deeper into those bank transactions, and now I wondered what we missed.

I snapped out of my thoughts as Xavier parked the car. We were both dressed down in sweats, when he came around to open my door, I couldn't help but to admire him. This strong man was fine as hell and always smelled good. His rich dark brown skin stayed moisturized. Stepping out the car, I interlocked our fingers. I wanted him to know I was riding with him no matter what we found out. He glanced down where our fingers meshed and smiled at me. "Nia, I know…"

"Don't. I told you because I wanted you to know how I feel. Not because I was looking for a response. When the time is right, you will get there," I said, looking up into those deep brown eyes to assure him. With everything going on, I understood him.

We walked straight toward the meeting room, and the strong scent of lavender slammed into my nostrils. We always kept lavender to calm our hostages before they were grilled. Today seemed like an extra boost was being pushed in to the air. "What the hell does Timothy have up his sleeve?" I said looking at Xavier.

Shrugging his shoulders, he walked into the room where we were greeted by Dad and a sad looking Jamilah.

"Hey, baby sis! What's going on, guys?" I looked strangely at my dad as we all exchanged hugs. I thought we decided to keep everyone out of this until we had come to a resolution.

"Y'all should have a seat. I looked into some things on Jerome Carter, and we found he is a habitual cheater," Timothy said and looked over at Xavier to gauge his response.

The tension in the room was thick, and I had a feeling it was going to get thicker.

"Xavier, we were looking into your dad and found out some things. We want to run some stuff by you before we bring him in here to fill in the holes."

Jamilah stood, taking a deep breath, then brushed her hands down her clothes. She walked over to Xavier, then asked, "Were you aware that your dad has had an affair with about twenty-five women? Possibly more." She looked deep in his eyes—searching for truth..

Xavier looked concerned, but he knew he needed to see it through and hear everything. He tried hard to keep his breathing steady as he knew they were watching closely. Jamilah seeing no deception in his face, she continued.

"One of those women happened to be Shirley Grant," Jamilah said. At once, X and I jumped up and yelled, "What?!".

Xavier started pacing back and forth whispering to himself. He finally asked, "When did this happen? Was it recent? Is it still going on?"

I just stood there helpless biting at my nails. My brain was struggling to process my mom having an affair with her husband's best friend. I noticed his natural calm aroma turned acrid and now gave off a scent of anxiety and panic. I felt helpless. I wanted to help, but what could I do?

Timothy stepped forward and answered the questions. "Based on the information we could gather, this happened over twenty plus years ago and is not still happening."

I released a breath I didn't know I was holding. Daddy continued speaking, "There is more that we need to tell you. Paternity for Jamilah is in question. I just discovered this information while researching who could be after your dad, Xavier. Jamilah put two and two together and asked your mother."

He turned to me to gauge my response. "Shirley wordlessly confirmed, he was her father."

That explains why Jamilah was missing a few family features.

The room was quiet as everyone processed this new information. Xavier looked deeply pained by all of this new information. My heart hurt for him. Life had turnt him every which way but loose these last few months. "This is all unfortunate, but how does this help us find out who is after Jerome and his family?" I couldn't take listening anymore. We needed real answers.

"Let's get Jerome up here," my dad said as they shared a knowing look. I just knew this was going to get worse. I didn't know if Xavier could handle any more news like this.

Chapter 19

Jerome Carter

B eing called out of the blue to go to the Onyx had my heart racing. Hopefully they found something so we could close this out. Stepping out of my Blue Metallic Audi A8 at the Onyx, the air was crisp, and the sun shined bright. I felt like a million bucks as I walked with my head held high. I was feeling on top of the world. I just knew my best friend would figure this shit out. He was *that* man when it came to finding and fixing stuff. I couldn't wait to hear this info and how they were going to handle it.

Instantly hit with a heaviness in the air as I walked in the building, my stomach dropped. "Uh, this doesn't look good. Hello, everyone! Why such long faces?"

Xavier sat at the head of the table with his head in his hands. He looked stressed. Nia sat quietly in a corner waiting for everything to unfold. Timothy stood by the door looking pissed.

Arms crossed, jaw clenched, and body unmoved, I felt like I had walked into the lion's den.

Tim started, "We are going to just come right out and give it to you straight."

His face was hardened, nostrils flaring. I now noticed the stress lines on my friend's face. This made my heart race. My palms were sweaty, the air stale, and now the room felt too small for everyone in attendance. "We created a list of all of your mistresses an-"

"Dad, what the fuck were you thinking?" Xavier yelled out interrupting Timothy in the midst of him delivering the news. "You betrayed your best friend? And now I may have a sister. I can't believe you. Does Mom know all of this?"

My mouth was stuck open as he chastised me like a child. I knew I was wrong for sleeping with Shirley, but what was he talking about a sister? Four sets of eyes shot to me waiting on a response. Silence. My face burned with shame. I turned toward Tim with a pleading tone. "Tim. I—"

"Save it, motherfucker." Timothy's voice cracked, the anguish audibly noticeable in his tone.

Jamilah stood up hesitantly and said, "That's not all. The man who wants you dead has evidence of you being tied to child sex trafficking."

Xavier jumped to his feet. "What? I know you lyin'." Nia rocked in the corner as she took in all this information looking between Xavier and his dad. I couldn't tell from her facial expression whether she wanted to pity me or kill me.

Timothy took a seat next to Xavier at the table shaking his head. "I don't even know you anymore. Sex trafficking?"

I was genuinely shocked as my body swayed slightly at the new discovery about myself. "Th—that is not true. I have done a lot of treacherous things, but I would never do anything like that." I looked down to my friend with pleading eyes hoping that he believed me.

"For your sake, I hope that's true, but honestly, I think its too late," Jamilah chimed in. Silence fell upon the room as everyone processed this new information. "I was asked to take you out during the New Year's party. Considering this new information, I thought I would wait to hear what you had to say."

"Wait. You have been the one hunting him? So, you were there? At the warehouse where Xavier was being held. I thought I scented you when we busted him out. How did you get tied up in this mess?" Timothy said.

"Well, since we are all laying it out on the line today. Shadow was the only one to believe that I could get active in the field. You never gave me a chance," she said with sheer determination as her body shook. "Maybe because I wasn't like you. Like your precious Nia," Jamilah said with pain in her voice. "It all makes sense now that the truth has come out. Why you treated me so different."

Jamilah stood to her feet, eyes glistening, to rush out and get fresh air when Timothy jumped to stop her. "Baby girl, I am sorry you felt this way. I never meant—" He choked on his words as tears formed. "I just wanted you to be ready, and with that extra layer of protection, I wouldn't have to worry about you out there. I know you are tough, but being a panther shifter gives you an added advantage."

Timothy's body stiffened, and the frightened expression stuck as he looked at Nia. I sat quietly, processing this new info. I had no clue what the hell they were talking about. There was so much I had to clear up.

"Guys, I am sorry to break this up, but I have a hit on my head and would like to fix this. I really am innocent." I cut in.

"Unfortunately, I don't think there is anything you can do. There is proof of you coordinating the transportation for the pick-up and drop off of the abducted kids. He wants you dead. Yesterday," Jamilah stated in a saddened tone.

"I coordinate transportation for another organization that moves medical equipment. I am not involved in child trafficking," I said, panicking. "You have to believe me. Aside from cheating on my wife, I am a respectable dude."

Everyone looked up at me like I had two heads after that statement. "Here, I will prove it to you."

I whipped out my phone from my pants pocket and sifted through my emails like a madman. "Found it." I showed Timothy an email from the first conversation about coordinating medical supply transportation.

Timothy kept the phone in his hand, looked over his glasses, and silently watched me. After a few moments of judgement and disdain seething from his pores, Timothy said dryly, "It appears you were being truthful at least once in your life." He then handed the phone over to the others to read the email. Xavier sat up straighter and let out a huge breath.

"This may be what we need to get them to call off the dogs," Nia said excitedly.

"It may be an uphill battle, but it's better than sitting around waiting to be killed," I stated in a jovial tone, grabbing on to Timothy's arm and shaking it. This would give me a chance to possibly mend some relationships and form others.

I couldn't believe that I had had a daughter. A sudden feeling of heaviness expanded in my core. I couldn't believe Shirley kept this from me. As I continued to wrap my mind around how I should move forward, whispers were heard throughout the room.

Not being able to worry about what they were talking about, I needed to talk to Jamilah. I walked to her as she talked to Timothy.

"Hey. Umm. I wanted to talk to you about this new infor—"

"Jerome, right now isn't a good time. I'll call you when I'm ready. This is a lot, and I just don't know."

She shook her head and walked away. Nia caught her at the door and blocked her exit. She apologized and tried to hug her, but Jamilah was over it. I know I messed up, but I never meant for a few nights of passion to go this far and affect this many.

I lost my best friend, my wife was probably going to kill me, and my son was disappointed. Priding myself in being my son's superhero, I tried to keep my disfunction far away from my family. I wanted him to be a much better man than me in every area. It seemeded I was successful in letting them all down. Hopefully, he gave me a chance to repair our relationship.

Turning to Xavier, I needed to speak to him alone. "Excuse me, Nia, could I have a moment with my son?" She looked like she was ready to rip my head off. I guess that was a good sign that she would do right by him. As she turned and walked out of the room, Xavier watched her every move. He had it bad already. I rubbed the back of my neck and blew out a long exhale. "You two seem serious. Are you sure about getting into something so serious this soon after Alissa? Especially now with you guys being practically family now." As I asked him about his new relationship, his face turned up in confusion.

"First off, Pops, you the last man to be giving somebody relationship advice. Second, there is no blood relations with Nia and I. I love her, and it ain't shit you can say to make me change how I feel."

He stopped talking abruptly. He looked deep in thought about something. "I love her? I love her."

He wasn't talking to me anymore. More like he was just realizing it himself.

"All I am saying is be careful. You see how her mom moves. She didn't even bother to tell me I had a kid walking around in this world."

He didn't even respond to me; he just kept this bewildered look on his face. Finally, he turned toward the door and walked out shaking his head.

"You should probably focus more on your relationship with Mama and Jamilah, than being worried about what I have going on. We good over here. She got me, and I damn sure got her. I plan to do a much better job than what you did with Mama."

He was right. And I hated myself for how right he was.

Chapter 20

Xavier

Walking out of the warehouse, I quickly decided I needed a drink. This shit had my blood pressure sky high. "I had survived the military, been shot at during a war and water boarded during training, but this takes the cake." Pacing back and forth, I shook my head at all of what had come out about my dad recently.

This man was my hero. I was supposed to be just like him. In my eyes, he could do no wrong. I worked hard to fit in those shoes. Dejected, I walked to the car with Nia and could not bring myself to engage much in conversation. How could this man be such a fraud?

"Babe, do you want to talk about it? I know that was a lot to take in all at once." Nia's voice was small and timid as she continued to drive through the city back to her place. The music was low and the tension in the car was so thick I know she wanted to let the window down so she could breathe.

"Naw, I'm good." I didn't want to be an asshole, but I truly didn't have the capacity to engage in a conversation about any of this shit. My thoughts were too loud to gain a moment of peace. After I told Nia I didn't want to talk about it, she gave me space to work things out mentally, but I replayed the events of today out on a loop in my head.

How was I supposed to move forward knowing that this "great man" in my life wasn't so great after all? Walking into Nia's house caused a calm in my spirit. I went to the guest room instead of Nia's bedroom to lay out. She wasted no time turning on her Housewives bullshit. Must mean I was stressing her out. I decided to just hop in the shower, get dressed and go eat. ALONE!

I didn't want my bad mood to ruin dinner for her. My dark cloud could just hover over me tonight. As I headed out, I realized that I needed to say...something to Nia. I don't know where I was going or for how long, but I was going. As I leaned down to kiss her forehead, she paused to look up in my eyes. Her softness. Her vulnerability broke my heart. At this moment I couldn't show up for her. Not like I wanted to. My shit was now bleeding over in to her world.

I briefly lost myself in her honey brown eyes. There was a glimmer of gold to come to the surface. Such intensity and strength shown. That moment I felt her love and the fight she had within. I know she would fight with me and for me. I just couldn't right now. Snapping out of the moment, I kissed her forehead and headed out the door.

I walked in to Lucky's Winsgspot for some drinks and basketball to clear my mind. Nia turned me on to this hidden gem, now I wanted to be hidden in it. I would deal with all of that other shit tomorrow. Ordering a whiskey neat, I sat at the bar and got lost in the game. College basketball would just have to do since it was still a little early. Professional games wouldn't start tonight until 7pm. Lucky's was pretty empty and quiet. The bartender dropped off my drink and didn't stay for small talk. I needed to make sure to tip him big when I left.

My wings came just in time to help soak up this liquor. As soon as I dug elbow deep in to my basket the chair beside me was pulled out and occupied by someone. Looking over to see who the hell would come sit their ass right beside me when the entire bar top was empty, I saw… Jamilah. My sister. What could she possibly want? How did she even know I was here?

Chewing my wings and fries, I chose not to verbally speak but nodded my head to say what's up. She smiled slightly then turned toward the TV. We sat in silence for a couple of minutes before she finally broke. "What do we do now?"

"I don't know. I guess it kind of depends. Are you going to kill your dad if your boss wants to keep the hit out on him?" I said flatly. More silence surrounded us.

"Xavier, I have no plans to carry out the hit on Jerome. That doesn't mean someone else won't go after him because of this new information. I was talking about us." She looked over to- ward me searching my face for answers. Answers that I don't have. As more silence surrounded us, I felt it was my turn to engage. "Wanna drink?"

"I'll take a Crown Apple and Cranberry. You buying food too?"

My eyes shot up to her and a slight chuckle escaped my mouth. "We haven't been siblings twenty-four hours, and you already trying to bleed my pockets."

Jamilah just laughed. After a few more rounds of drinks and eventually being suckered in to getting her wings we decided to call it a night. Standing to my feet, I stretched out my arms and yawned. It was time to hit the bed. "Jamilah, I know this is all messed up, but I have no intentions on ignoring you as my sibling. Once we figure out this mess, maybe we can hang again. Let me walk you to your car."

She packed her things up and we walked to her Mercedes AMG. "You be safe getting home," I told her as I closed her door. I felt better, and now I needed to be up under my girl. I walked to my car and before I could climb in I heard the distinct sound of glass shattering. I dropped to the ground to hopefully get a better view of where the shot came from. By this time, the sun was down, and visibility wasn't as good as earlier. This was the perfect condition to execute a hit. Unfortunately, they were still coming at me to try to smoke him out his hiding spot.

The sound of tires screeching made my ears perk up in alert. "Get in the car!" Jamilah screamed through the window. As soon as I tried to stand to my feet, the shots rang out again. Jumping in, Jamilah sped off before I slammed the door shut. We peeled out of the parking lot and made a left on the busy street blowing right through an intersection. She definitely drove the shit out of this car. The stick shift didn't slow her down one bit. We hit a corner and sped up trying to get away from whoever was shooting at me.

"Looks like I need to make that call to my boss sooner rather than later."

"No shit, Sherlock," I practically yelled out as she made another turn to the right. A few shots rang out from behind us and I swear she kicked the car in to overdrive. This little ass car had more power than I knew.

"You could shoot back or something, you know."

"Well, I didn't have any plans to be in an episode of Bad Boys, so I apologize if I am unprepared."

She glanced at me and rolled her eyes with a half smile. "Shadow, I need you to call off the hit on Jerome. I have some news for you that you are going to want to see. It changes everything," Jamilah said nervously as our speeds elevated. I looked at her face as she continued the conversation with Shadow. Even though I could only hear her side of the phone conversation, I felt good about our options. We switched lanes and went airborne over railroad tracks. My head slammed on the ceiling of the car as I yelled, "You are going to kill me before they do."

"What is he saying? Where are we going? I swear if you are kidnapping me again—"

"Would you calm down? I am handling it." When she looked over at me, briefly, my heart was relieved. This was the weirdest bonding session ever. We pulled into the underground parking lot of the Onyx. My breathing was finally returning to normal when Jamilah jumped out of the car still talking to Shadow. What ever she was saying had calmed down the shooting, and I was ever grateful. Nia was going to be pissed.

Should I even tell her? Feeling trapped on what to do, I suddenly needed water for my cotton mouth. I had never pissed a panther off, so I was mildly frightened for my safety. She was little but dangerous. I knew how extensive their training was with Timothy and didn't want to be on her bad side. Chewing the inside of my lip, I bit the bullet and decided to call Nia. I had been gone a while, she was probably going to think I ran away.

"Hey, baby, I'm fine, but somebody came after me at Lucky's. Yes, again! Jamilah was there and brought me to the Onyx. I just wanted to tell you where I was so you wouldn't worry."

"I'll come get you. You can get your car from Lucky's in the morning," Nia responded with an exasperated tone.

Chapter 21

Nia

I sat in my bedroom right in the middle of my bed. The house was dark except the candles were lit and my mood lights were shining bright. Dinner tonight would be popcorn and wine. Since Xavier went out for dinner, I didn't see the need to slave over the stove for an elaborate meal. I took a quick shower, did my night routine, and put on my sexy negligee for when my man made it back home. He had had a lot thrown at him and what better way to free his body of the stress than to drain him until exhaustion. After 4 episodes of *Housewives of Blackwater Bay* I began to fidget with my phone and the remote.

Here I was, laid here looking sexy and ready to be devoured, but X was no where to be found. Had he changed his mind about us? Maybe this was all too much for him. I did just drop a major bomb on him. Two. Telling someone you loved them could be big, especially after what he went through. His trust issues were at an all time high. Now this new discovery with his dad. A sister. My sister. How do we even navigate that? I mean its not like we are blood related but still, its...different. "I'm just going to end it with him." I said ou tloud to myself. This was all too much for one person to handle. He was so inundated with shit he had to run away to wherever he was, to clear his mind. My mood shifted as I thought about walking away from him. I finally found someone, but apparently it wasn't in the cards for me. Walking into the kitchen to put away my food, my phone rung in the bedroom. I sprinted back to catch the phone. This better be X calling to tell me something and it better be good.

"Again?!! I'll come get you. You can get your car from Lucky's in the morning." I huffed out. I was going to kick his ass. "Oh, let's just go galavanting in the city like there is no one out to kill you and your family," I said, snatching my keys off the table, rolling my eyes. I changed clothes into sweats to pick him up from the Onyx Hunt. I was grateful that he was not hurt, but this could have been avoided. I slammed my stuff down on to the conference table when I got to our warehouse. Standing with my arms crossed, I waited for answers to questions I didn't think I needed to ask. Jamilah walked in with an unreadable expression. We haven't talked since everything came out with Jerome. She basically ignored my calls.

"I have a meeting Monday with the big boss. I will go over the new info Jerome gave us. I am still going to try to find out the contacts for the shell company to see if we can get a schedule or something. Maybe we can intercept a transport and save some kids. That will sweeten the pot for the big boss to call off the hit on Jerome. Until then you and your family need to just continue to lay low."

While it wasn't what I wanted to hear, it was better than bad news. "Thanks, sis, for jumping in tonight," I stated. X and I stood silently then headed for the door. He turned to her and held his hand out to shake.

"Thank you for saving my ass tonight. I almost had them." She stood there silent with her mouth wide open as he walked toward the door. I didn't know what that was about, but something was telling me that he indeed did *not* almost have them. I drove us back to the house and didn't press the issue on getting answers. What was important was that he was not harmed and when he was ready to open up he would. I am a safe space for him and would hold room for him to work on his own timing. He afforded me that luxury, and I could reciprocate.

The next morning, I completed my morning routine when I noticed Xavier never came to my room. He slept in the guest bedroom. He was still laid out on the bed even thought the sun was out and shining bright. This was causing my panther to get restless. She was fearful that he would reject us like the rest of them. She kept me up most of the night. I didn't even have an appetite for breakfast.

I needed to go for a run. That should help calm my panthers nerves, at least for now. My panther wanted Xavier and would be devastated if this didn't work out. Heading to the back yard

I stepped through the glass door and took in the clean and fresh air. The sun was illuminating my face and activating this melanin. The wind caused the scene of the forest to be serene and peaceful. I was overwhelmed with excitement to get in the trees and relax my mind. The forest gives me a peace that a bubble bath and wine could never.

I shifted into my panther mid-air as I jumped from the porch. The stretch of my limbs created a euphoric feeling in my body that reminded me I don't do this enough. With each step I took, the weight of the world loosened its grip, melting into the rhythm of my stride. I ran until my limbs were tired then I laid in my favorite place—by the stream. The quiet serenity of the tranquillizing stream and the luminous vibrancy of the water kept my eyes transfixed.

Suddenly, I scented something warm, spicy. The smell engulfed my senses and soon I saw the reason. Xavier continued to walk toward me as I laid out in the sun. I didn't bother moving. He found a log close by and sat on it watching the stream in silence. "Are we still going to your family's house for Sunday dinner?" he said abruptly. I guess he was more comfortable with my panther than I realized. I stood, sashayed toward him, rubbed my body against his leg, then plopped down by his feet.

He reached down to stroke my coat, and a purr from the depths of my chests flew from my lips. His body stiffened, then a chuckle that melted my heart came from X. My panther was in pure bliss. This time with her mate would not be prematurely interrupted by a dinner. Their bond was growing, and he seemed at peace in the midst of the chaos.

Our peaceful time of solitude was ending. We needed to head back to the house before darkness overtook our space. Then head to my parents' home for Sunday dinner. Well, we were going to pretend it was Sunday since they canceled it earlier this week. This should be interesting with the new info. How would my overly dramatic mother respond to us knowing about her infidelity? She never took accountability for any wrongdoing. The only difference tonight would be that we all knew, and she wouldn't be able to pop-off on Xavier if things started spiraling out of her control. She wouldn't be able to use her tears and guilt us into letting it go. Unfortunately, I felt things would come to a head tonight.

Chapter 22

Xavier

I enjoyed sitting out by the stream with Nia's panther, relaxing. I felt surprisingly closer to her Panther after our time together. Now, as we walked back to our house—wait, *OUR* house. When did it become our house? I could see myself with Nia long term, but it would have to be after this mess was cleared up. Right now, I wasn't good enough. I needed to be my best self for her, but she has become my best friend. Aside from the panther secret, she was a completely open book to me. She had come a long way with opening up with me. I got to see the mess that was Nia. I got to see experience the perfect imperfection of her world.

She deserved my best self, and I planned to give it to her, right now just was not the right time. Nia shifted back and walked in to the house to dress for the dinner. I knew this dinner would be different from the others but I plan to face whatever happens head on.

We pulled up to Nia's family home. As I put the car in park, I stopped and blew out a deep breath. By the looks of it, everyone was here, probably waiting on us to eat. We walked in to the immaculately decorated dining area, and all eyes turned to greet us in the doorway.

"Hello, everyone!" I waved as I walked in and took my seat. Mr. Grant made his way to give me a bro hug and said a prayer over the food. As we dug in, Ms. Shirley started up, as to be expected.

"Nia, you look.... comfortable today. Did you just roll out of the bed?"

The room paused as everyone waited for a reply. The tension in the room was thicker than cold peanut butter. I looked over to see how Nia was going to handle this situation, when I noticed a red hue on her cheeks. I grabbed her hand under the table to help ground her and keep her from spiraling.

She pushed out a tight smile and said, "Mother, I am here with family. Hanging with family is a casual affair, and I am tired from recent events. There was no need to put on an act to sit and eat with my family."

She finished making her plate and held her head high. I was proud of my baby. She didn't crack under the constant scrutiny of her mother.

Sitting straighter in her seat Shirley replied, "Well, what if you had to make a stop on the way back home? People will look at you and think you were homeless. Do you want them to think we have raised daughters to look homeless?" She scoffed then turned her entire body away from Nia after that statement.

Nia rolled here eyes and mumbled under her breath, "Better for people to think I'm homeless than a home wrecker."

My eyes widened at her statement, but no lies were told. Timothy heard Nia as well and choked on his chicken, laughing as the entire table sat in shock. You could hear a rat piss on cotton in the dining area. No one was talking but the silence was loud. I felt like a proud Papa next to her.

Dinner went on in silence. No one knew what to say after that bomb had been dropped. Aaliyah and Keisha sat in confusion the entire meal because they had not been filled in yet from the new discoveries. I heard a few phones chime during the meal, and I could only guess they were asking in one of their group chats. When dinner was complete, Shirley didn't waste time getting out of that dining room. She left the clean up to everyone else. One thing I noticed, Mr. Timothy did nothing to save her. I hoped they could recover from such a great betrayal.

After dinner, Timothy and I went into his Man Cave to watch a game. We mostly sat in silence as the game played. Timothy had his Old Fashion in hand when he decided to sit up in his chair. "So, are you and Nia going to continue with this arrangement once we get everything cleared up? By the looks of everything, you two look good for each other."

He sat back in his chair but still watched me intently. Sipping on his drink, he sat silently as I mentally processed his words.

"Mr. Timothy," I huffed out a long exhale as I rubbed my hand over my waves.

"Son, you're going to have to get over that mess. Your daddy made that bed. Not you. Don't allow his mess to affect your life." He took a sip of his drink then chuckled at me. "Don't let a good woman pass you by worried about a temporary situation being stressed out by somebody else's bullshit. It's not even your situation.

"Now if you can't be a man and stand ten toes down for my baby, walk away now. I would hate to put you in a body bag later for being like your daddy."

We both laughed when he looked at me with one eyebrow raised. He walked over and clapped his hand on my shoulder. There was a lot to think about. Timothy was right, I would be heated to see another man with Nia later.

The car ride home was rather silent as well. I knew Nia was in her head overthinking tonight's events. Taking it upon myself to break her out of what, I am sure, was a spiral of negative thoughts I grabbed her thigh while I drove. The demonstrated strength of my woman was commendable and had been since we first met, teaching me a resilience I had never known. She was deserving of the world, and I planned to give it to her.

I knew we were going to have to sit down with Shirley and my dad soon. I needed Nia there to be my peace. I knew now I needed her in my life as my wife, The mother of my kids, or... baby cats. I didn't want to wait. There was nothing left to think about. She was it for me. Thinking hard about Nia caused my crotch to swell in my pants. We couldn't get home fast enough. Reaching over, I grabbed her hand and placed it in my lap. She looked in my eyes, and a devilish grin appeared on her face.

"What were you over there thinking about to cause this situation?" she said grinning.

"You. And how I'm about to work you overtime. I'm talking... I want you spread open for me so I can show you my appreciation," my voice dropped a few octaves as I told her the plans. We pulled up to our home, and I ran to her side of the car to carry her inside. The night was still young, and I was ready to pull an all nighter.

Chapter 23

Jamilah

Heading to my family's house for Wednesday dinner had me a little on edge. This would be our first time all together after the news broke. My mom would be on her bullshit, as usual, making the night about her in some way. My phone rung as I exited the car to head inside.

"Hey! We have another player in the city. I know you asked me to pause the "order" until I hear you out, but they were already here. I just wanted to give you a head's up."

The dark, ominous voice of Shadow blared through my phone and left me too stunned to speak. My heart began to race, and my body heat a few degrees. "Depending on this new info you have for me, I will consider canceling my order. But, Jamilah, this better be damn good."

I finally found my voice and said, "Y-yes, I think you would be happy to see this new development. T-tomorrow at 10am, right?"

My voice so uncertain, I barely recognized it myself.

"Yes, 10am, if his alarm clock still rings in the morning."

Then the phone disconnected. That last statement sent shivers down my spine causing pain in my head and my limbs. The stress of this case had my body reacting crazy. Cracking my neck from side to side, I hoped it would relieve some stress. I held my head high and turned on the charm for dear ole Mommy dearest as I walked through the door.

"Hello, people!" I walked in to the living room where the twins were sitting gossiping about something. After hugging them, I went in to the kitchen to look for the parentals. The sizzling bacon smell greeted me at the door, and my stomach instantly growled. A woozy feeling came over me, and suddenly, I was as hungry as a starving animal.

Dang, I should have eaten breakfast.

Daddy sat at the marble top kitchen island drinking his whiskey on ice while Mama worked her magic with the pots. As she pulled something out of the oven, my sense of smell was overwhelmed with the sweet deliciousness of golden-brown cornbread. My vision blurred, and I quickly spoke, then went off to lay down after stealing a piece of bacon. She won't miss a piece or two. This bacon was for the collard greens she was washing in the sink, but my body needed them right now.

I ventured down the long dark hallway to lay in a bed in one of the guest bedrooms. Stopping in the bathroom to dash water on my face, the lights were too bright to stand. I noticed a slight glow in my eyes. It was as if I was looking in the mirror as it was looking into me. "I must be hallucinating due to hunger. Let me lay my ass down," I said softly to myself.

A few hours passed, when Daddy came in to wake me from my slumber. I noticed the lines around his eyes. The secrets, the betrayal, and the stress weighed heavy on him. This was not a look that sleep could cure. His soul was tired.

We all sat around the table and just as we were about to say grace over the food, in walked Nia and Xavier. I mumbled, "This has to be the weirdest shit ever."

Looking around the table to see if anyone heard me, I noticed Keisha and Aaliyah looking confused. They were so out of the loop with the happenings of this dysfunctional family, it was crazy.

The show started right after we said our prayers over the food. Mom couldn't wait to dig into one of her girls. The lucky victim tonight was little Ms. Perfect. As I devoured this meal, my mind zoned out to all conversations until I noticed the air shift in the room. Nia tried to mumble under her breathe, but I heard her, "Better for people to think I'm homeless than a home wrecker."

Oh, shit! Not Ms. Put-together stepping off her throne to get somebody together.

That little comment shut my mother up so fast, I had forgotten she was in the room by the time we finished up. The girls were texting in our group chat to see what the hell was going on, but this was definitely a conversation needed over mimosas. We cleaned the kitchen together while the guys went into the Man Cave to talk. Settling in to a quiet rhythm, Nia apologized to me as I dried the dishes. "Why are you apologizing?"

"As your big sister, I was supposed to know what's going on and how you felt. I wanted to support you. I didn't understand how you felt, but I could have been there to at least listen. I could have brought the vodka," she said with a chuckle. We stood shoulder-to-shoulder, and she slid over to bump my shoulder. " In spite of how you felt about all of this and me, I do love you! Hell, I don't even *want* to be the head of the Onyx Hunt when Daddy retires. AND we need you. You are important to our family and the organization."

She continued to talk while I just listened. Tears welled up in my eyes as she poured her heart out about everything. This conversation was everything I didn't know I needed. Throughout all of this, I felt abandoned and not good enough. She cleared that misconception tonight. Especially when she talked about dad and his epic fail at trying to do my job. We laughed so hard, my stomach hurt. She jumped suddenly and stilled her body.

My eyesight blurred and head hurt again. I grabbed the counter to balance myself in the kitchen. Nia asked, "Do you feel OK? You don't look good."

I didn't feel good either. The words were trapped inside as my body ached. My bones cracked, and my head throbbed. Nia yelled for my dad to come in the kitchen as I collapsed on the floor. The world went dark as I saw my family gathering around me.

Awaking outside on the ground was different. *Why the hell am I on the ground?* I heard people talking, but the sound was muffled. Suddenly, the clean scent of freshly mowed grass overpowered my senses, causing me to become nauseous. The cool breeze of the Florida night danced across my skin, each hair rising as if it, too, had come alive. Whatever happened in the kitchen caused a heightened sensory awakening.

In the blink of an eye, I was staring face to face with a large panther with bold and bright silver eyes. Silver eyes? Dad? He began to speak to me, but...in my mind.

Babygirl, you finally shifted. Stand to your feet. Balance your-self—feel the earth beneath you.

As I tried to stand, I felt like a baby deer on wobbly legs walking for the first time. I looked around to see my entire family standing around admiring me...my panther. The prickle of the grass under my panther's paws titillated my senses. With a thrill coursing threw my veins, I shot out of the backyard into the forest.

From the edge of the forest, I could see dead leaves and pine needles caught in clumps of moss for miles deep. The mustiness of the moss tickled my nose as I sped past tall trees rising out of the earth that looked as if they could brush the sky. A heavy swell in my chest exploded when I looked over to see that beautiful coal black, shiny coat and those oh so bright silver eyes sparkling like stars. My daddy. His panther was running with me. This was something I had waited for all of my life. No other event could top tonight's feelings. We headed back to the family home where I was met with a reflection of myself.

My coat was a satiny black with dark gray spots, almost like a camouflage. My eyes glowed a champagne color, and my form was large but not nearly as large as my dad. His panther glided toward me, brushing his powerful body against mine. A low, vibrating chuff rumbled from his chest—deep, steady, and full of reassurance. Shifting back into my human form, I was able to end my night, heart fully satisfied.

Waking up Thursday morning, I felt a renewed spirit. The sun illuminated intensely through my bedroom window. I hopped out of bed to prepare for this crucial meeting with Mr. Big Boss man, Shadow. I had to make sure I was on top of my game if I planned to save Jerome's life. With this new player in the city—time was crucial. We needed the hit order canceled immediately if he had any chances of surviving the week. We knew of one player in the city, but who knew how many were gunning for him in the shadows?

Laid out on my bed was a hunter green pantsuit—a symbol of a quiet warrior, calm yet commanding, moving with purpose. If I wanted to have any chance of building a relationship with my father, I had to first keep him alive. Double checking my bag, I confirmed I had all the evidence needed to convince Shadow to spare his life. Then I had to decide if I was going to work with the Marceau Foundation, or did I stick with the Onyx Hunt?

I pulled up to the warehouse, and it was quiet. Too quiet. My panther was on edge, and my palms were sweaty. I blew out a big breath then exited the car.

"Head high, chin up, girly. You can do this." I gave myself a pep talk as I walked in the door. We met in the large conference room and I laid out all of my documents for Shadow to see as soon as he walked in.

Walking in with the ego of a king, Shadow sat at the head of the conference table with an unreadable expression. Before I was able to begin, he stated, "I see you have not been able to take out the target. You better have a good reason as to why you couldn't execute. Are you not cut out for this line of work?"

He paused and glared in my eyes like he was seeing through to my soul.

"I don't think you should be going after Jerome Carter. He was a pawn to receive transport. His impression was that it was medical supplies. We have screenshots of the original email sent requesting the services right here."

I passed him the documents then stepped back to watch him process it all.

"Do we know who this company is, or was he just interested in the money he would make?" His voice boomed through the room.

"Yes, after a little digging, the original name that was given to Jerome was just a shell company to hide under. The real organization belongs to a Dallas Moon with Moon Productions. He not only transported the children, his production company filmed them and sell it across the globe. My chest tightened as those words left my mouth. By the looks of it, this new news didn't quite create a warm feeling for Shadow either.

Shadow stood and slammed his hands on the oakwood table. The loud thunderous boom caused my heart to throb. I think I pee'd a little. He was enraged by the news. "Give me a few minutes. I will cancel the order on Jerome."

He walked toward the door but paused and turned back. "I'm glad the truth came out about your real dad. Now you both have a second chance to build a relationship. Oh, and good looking out on the hit. This new info should give us an opportunity to hit bigger fish in this disgusting game."

Sitting there looking crazy with my mouth wide open, and my face turned up, all I could do was be grateful. In the midst of the storm, the sun shined bright on me. I shifted for the first time, worked things out with my sister, and my panther ran with my dad's panther. No matter what, that man was still my daddy. My hero.

I hopped back into the Benz and could finally breathe. My cheeks hurt from the large smile on my face. Before I pulled off, my phone rang, and Daddy's name showed up on the console.

"Hey, babygirl!" boomed through my speakers.

"What's going on, Daddy?"

"I called to see if you thought more about our conversation. You staying with the Onyx Hunt. We need you."

I tried my hardest not to laugh and yell as I heard, "I want to also offer you a position as Huntress. You have proven even in your human form that you can do this. Now I know you can. Also, family panther run Saturday at 8am." I rolled my eyes, but deep inside, I couldn't be happier.

"Yes, Daddy! I am staying with Onyx. Shadow's organization is cool, but it's not family." We laughed a little more as I pulled out of the parking lot. Things were definitely looking up for me.

Chapter 24

Shirley

"Shirley, I don't want to talk about this shit right now. You cheated, you lied, you got pregnant, and lied some more. You would have continued to lie if we had not found out. So, no, I don't want to spend time with your lying ass. You had twenty five years to come clean, and you didn't. So, excuse me if I need more time to "get over it"," Timothy said with a tired voice.

He sat at the bar with yet another drink in hand. Since the news broke, that's all he seemed to have time to do.

I pleaded with Timothy, "I know, and I am sor—"

"You are just sorry you got caught, Shirley. You don't give a damn about nobody else but yourself."

He slumped his shoulders while he continued to nurse his whiskey. I noticed his hand partially shifted around the glass. He was fighting to keep his panther inside.

"Now, that's a damn lie. I sacrificed so much for you and this entire family."

My body trembled, and my eyes began to glow a blazing champagne as I yelled at him. "I sacrificed my career so that we could begin a family. Sacrificed my body so that we could keep trying until we had a boy. I sacrificed my time, but you never wanted to retire. I sacrificed my happiness because you needed the perfect little stay at home wife. I sacrificed who I was, and nobody noticed."

I paced the living room, memories pulling me back to the days when our kids were small. "What did I get in return?" I yelled. "Diamonds! Cars! Vacations! All I ever wanted was *you*. Was that too much to ask for."

I took a deep breath to calm myself. This wasn't like me. I didn't yell. Calmly, I said, "I had to always be put together when I stepped out of the house because I was the great Timothy Grant's wife. I had to work extra hard to not be in your shadows and only be known as Timothy Grant's wife."

Walking close and getting in his face, I looked in his eyes. He needed to feel my words. "Why do you think I had to be the hostess with the best parties? The socialite? Then you were always gone—"

The doorbell rung interrupting our much needed conversation. As Timothy walked to open the door, my breathing stopped. Jerome and Barbara walked into the living room. I couldn't believe Timothy set me up like this. He invited them over and left me in the dark. Moving to the dark gray plush couch to sit opposite of the Carters, I held my head high and prepared my mind for what was to come.

"I called you all here so we can get some answers from you two," Timothy slurred his words as he pointed to Shirley and Jerome. "I would like to know why my best friend and my wife thought it would be a good idea to sleep together, then hid it for years."

Timothy was trembling as those words fell from his lips.

"I always knew you were jealous."

Barbara sat on my couch with a smug face and judged me. I wasn't jealous of her, nor did I ever want Jerome. The sex was good, and I was lonely, but of course, I couldn't say that. "You worked so hard to throw your accomplishments in my face every chance you got. I knew you weren't a real friend; I just never knew it was this bad."

She turned around to Jerome and just shook her head. "Do you hate me that much? You slept with someone in our circle? Your best friend's wife. What is wrong with you?"

Tears welled up in my eyes as I experienced the hurt and pain caused from my selfishness. "There are no amount of words to express how sorry I am to the both of you. Tim, I was alone. A lot. You were away with the military or off handling Onyx Hunt business. You left me alone with four small children. A lot." I huffed. Hurt and disappointment settled in my chest. "I never meant to hurt either of you. We saw each other coincidentally during one girls trip, and it just happened." My voice trailed away.

Shame covered my face as I continued. "This rendezvous continued until I got pregnant. I knew the baby was Jerome's based off the timing. I tested Jamilah as well using Nia. She was not a 100 percent match, which told me she did not belong to Timothy."

Barbara jumped up and blurted, "How do you know if Jerome is her father? You were sleeping with men outside of your marriage."

My blood boiled at the accusation thrown at me. My champagne eyes glimmered, my panther ready to pounce on Barbara and tear her apart limb by limb. As the classy lady that I am, I kept my head held high and refuted the allegations.

"Barbara, I know you are hurt by our actions, but please believe I am not a loose woman. I've only slept with Jerome outside of my marriage. Mind you, this was over twenty years ago. We have not been intimate in nearly twenty years. If he has been unfaithful since then, it was not with me."

As if that made it better, I had to notify her. Turning to my husband, I grabbed his hands and placed them in my lap. "I truly apologize. I love you with everything in me." I paused to let him process my words.

"After my indiscretions, I realized I wanted my family above all else. That is why I stayed when I wanted to run. My girls needed their father, all of my girls. And I needed my husband.

I felt if I could just hold out until you retired, things would be perfect. I knew you loved me. Hopefully, you still love me," I said softer, looking into his unreadable expression. Oh my! I think I may have lost my husband. His heart was so hard toward me.

"What you and Jerome did was pretty unforgivable. Not only did you have an affair, you had a kid. Shirley, you doubled down and lied to everyone about it. Did you ever pause to think about Jamilah and how it would affect her?"

Timothy looked at Jerome with pained eyes. "Do you plan to be a part of Jamilah's life? Keep in mind, she will FOREVER be my babygirl. I just think it's right to allow you the opportunity, but don't play with her heart. Her mom did that enough."

He shot daggers at me as he spoke to his former best friend.

Jerome responded, "Yes, if she will allow me to." He looked to me as if I could throw him a lifeline.

Obviously, there were more things that couldn't be worked out in front of Jerome and Barbara, but I was willing to fight for my marriage. As we walked them to the door, Jerome turned to Timothy with a pleading look. "I looked at you like my brother. Although I never meant to hurt you, I see I have. I am sorry. To you and my wife. If you will find it in your heart, I would like to move past this twenty-year-old indiscretion."

Timothy clenched his jaw as his friend spoke casually about the incident. He grabbed the handle of the large twelve-foot door and yanked it open. He said, "Man, get out of my house before I rip your throat out with my bare hands."

Without hesitation, Jerome and Barbara quickly left our home. My husband slammed the door and walked back to our bedroom. This was killing me inside to have the love of my life hurting, even worse, I was the cause of the pain. Seems I had been the source of pain for my husband and all my girls.

With a heavy heart, I headed to our bedroom. Stopping in my tracks, I was at a loss for words. Was Timothy packing a suitcase? He was leaving.

What do I do now? I can't lose him. I just really got him back.

Heading in his direction, he looked up with all the damage and strain written on his face.

"Shirley, I'm leaving. I can't. I know you felt abandoned in the beginning of our marriage, but this is too much. I am going to get a room for a few days."

He walked out of the bedroom, the house, but not out of my heart. I would get my husband back...

Chapter 25

Nia & X

After our last sex session, I received a call from Jamilah about an assignment. I dreaded it but peeled myself from X and dressed to kill. Changes needed to be made soon about my work schedule. If Xavier and I were going to continue with our relationship, I needed to cut back on my midnight activities. He hadn't said anything, but I could know he was not too fund of waking up in the middle of the night and I was gone.

As I reached my location, an illegal game room on the border of Blackwater and Miramar, I heard patrons leaving.

"Alright, Malik. See your grumpy ass later. Stay out of trouble," two bear shifters joked with each other as they headed out. They were some of the biggest shifters I had ever seen. Finally, my target decided to leave out with an escort. I knew I needed to make it quick to get back home to my man. There was something different about him. I scented something primal... wildlife like. This particular target had been found to be embezzling money from the city, more so the underserved communities in the Miramar Isles. So, not only was he stealing money, he was taking it from a population with nothing to spare.

Stalking over to his vehicle, I partially shifted and punctured the back tires on his pearl white GMC truck. He was sloppy drunk and didn't even notice the back was lower. He brought the truck to a loud grumble when he turned the key in the ignition, and right as he was pulling forward, he noticed. Throwing his truck into park, he jumped out to assess the problem.

I shifted into my panther and stalked toward my target. He glanced up as if he scented me. I noticed his eyes turn an unnatural blue, then he shifted into a wolf. The growl from his throat was like none other I had ever heard before. He was now in a full sprint toward me as I braced for impact. As he launched in the air, I crouched down to meet his under carriage. Aiming for his throat, I missed but caught his chest. He was quick, but I was quicker. Stepping back from my attack, he launched his body into mine, throwing me into the side of a car. My panther was hurt but not broken.

With a few nips at my legs, he had drawn blood. I knew I needed to end this before things got out of hand. With a paw to his face, my claws tore into his flesh. A whine from him let me know he was injured. I raised another paw to slash at him again as he tried to retreat. This was perfect. A little game of cat and mouse. As I continued to use my claws for assault, he was being weakened. Tiring of this game, I charged at him, aiming for his neck again, this time catching his flesh with my teeth. I yanked once, twice, and the third time, I pulled his throat away from his body. The target had been neutralized.

I tried to sneak back in the house and was caught red handed. This man saw me covered in someone else's blood from head to toe. As I limped in the house I passed him silently, he stopped me in my tracks. He assessed my injuries but stayed quiet. Xavier knew what all my job entailed. He grabbed my hand and led me to the bathroom to clean me up.

No words needed to be spoken. As I let him take care of me physically, I realized I had let this man fully into my heart. As I laid in the oversized tub, he wiped the blood from my face. He sat on the ledge of the marble tub and leaned in to kiss my forehead. "I love you, Nia. I accept all parts of you."

He sat and looked through to my soul. I allowed him to bathe my body, dry me, oil my skin, and carry me to bed. This man had pushed past all my walls and pierced my heart.

Xavier had taught me more in a few months than I ever would have imagined. He taught me to be authentically myself despite how others might judge me. For that, I was grateful. He rode for me just as hard as I did for him. He had me covered in prayer, positive affirmations, and love. And I'd be damned if I let him go uncovered, mentally, physically, or emotionally.

The day had come. It was time to lay it all on the line with my dad. As we walked into the comfort of my family home, I was hit with a wave of nausea. The stench of betrayal made my stomach turn. Walking past all the family pictures in the long hall way, I shook my head. An overwhelming feeling of my life being a lie caused me to stumble. Nia noticed and grabbed my hand for added reassurance.

When my dad walked into the modestly decorated living room, I sat back and reminisced on the version of him I created in my imagination. I realized he was a flawed human being outside of being my father. I had to come to grips with that new realization.

"Hey, Pops! How is everything?"

He walked directly to me and stood chest to chest with me as to assess my thoughts and feelings. Finally, he reached out to hug me and whispered an apology in my ear. No one was perfect, but I was not letting him off the hook. As we began talking about everything, Nia decided to head to the backyard to enjoy a little quiet sunshine. She was in my direct line of sight, so I was not too worried about her. Digging right in on the what and the why, I asked my dad if he planned on doing the right thing and building a relationship with Jamilah.

"She is actually pretty cool, Dad. We sat at the bar at Lucky's Wingspot, drank, watched the game, and she bled my pockets with all the food she ordered."

We both sat back with a hearty laugh. "Honestly, I always wanted a sister. Just not like this. How is Mom taking it?"

"You know how she is. A shopping spree or a trip, and all was forgiven," he said with a shrug of his shoulders. That wasn't my business, so I left it alone. I realized, though, that was not the type of relationship for me. They were just existing with each other. No love, no support, no commitment. I was definitely good on that. This world was too treacherous to be out here alone. I loved coming home to a woman that cared about me and my well-being. Then when she wrapped them chocolate legs around me, things were right in my soul.

"Well, Dad, we are going to head out. I have a brunch date with a beautiful lady who raises my heart rate."

I chuckled as I stood to walk to the backyard. Nia was laying in the hammock with a mimosa and an e-book. Who knew what freaky ass book she was reading now, probably some crazy shit about aliens with ten dicks that rotated. As I helped her out of the hammock, I quickly captured her sweet lips in a deep kiss to remind us both of what we were building.

Driving down the highway to the restaurant, I opened the panoramic sunroof and intertwined our fingers. This feeling deep in my chest was a mix of love and determination. We had both weathered some crazy things here recently, and I wouldn't change the journey if it led me to Nia every time. She released my hand and rubbed the back of my head stroking through the waves. This was the life I needed for the rest of my life.

Epilogue

Keisha

Rushing across the street to beat the oncoming traffic, I hurried into Lucky's Wingspot to grab some of their famous spinach dip that my family loved.

"Thank you!" I said shyly and blushed as I walked past the big chocolatey something holding open the door. His eye contact was intense when he said, "You're welcome, beautiful. I would love to get to know you. What's your name?"

Who the hell was this person running my body? When did I become shy? The words were caught in my throat as I extended my hand. "My name is Keisha."

"Well, Ms. Keisha, the first time I met you, I said I would get your number the next time we ran across each other. Would you let me take you out?" He dug in his pocket then passed me his phone to input my number.

"Well, sir, I don't even know your name. I don't just go out with strangers. You could be a killer or something."

I chuckled and noticed he just smiled. His hazel-colored eyes pinned me in place, and my heart rate sped up. My panther was intrigued.

"My name is Lucien. You are definitely safe with me, pretty lady. Now that I have your number, we can schedule something for tomorrow, if you are available."

"I would like that. I'm headed to a family cookout, so let me get in here and grab my contribution."

"So, you can't cook is what you're saying?" he said, throwing his head back in a hearty laugh.

"Ha-Ha! I am a busy woman keeping the streets of Blackwater safe. "

He tilted his head to the side as I spoke. "Impressive! Don't let me hold you up from the family dinner. I'll call you later tonight."

Epilogue

Jamilah

"Hey, Daddy! How you holding up?" I sat at the patio table drinking my margarita Nia made. Daddy leaned in to hug me and kiss my forehead before he sat down and lit his cigar.

"Hey, babygirl!! You know me. Anyway, I wanted to run something by you. I talked to Xavier, Nia is looking to pull back slightly with the Onyx. I need your commitment to take over as the lead Midnight Huntress. Xavier may be taking over my position after tonight's announcement. She will still take on jobs, you will just be lead. The workload is more, but I think you can handle it. What say you?"

He sat back in his seat, crossed his legs over the other, and waited.

My heart exploded with joy as I jumped out of my seat into his lap for the biggest hug and kiss I could muster. "I thought you would never ask. Of course, Daddy!"

He laughed like a big kid as I showered him with kisses all over his face. It was so good to hear a genuinely happy sound leave his mouth. After the big blow up with Mom, things were really gray for him. She was working overtime to get him back, too, and he was enjoying every minute of it.

She had also reached out to me to apologize profusely. I didn't understand her reasons for everything she did, but I loved my worrisome mother, and I wouldn't trade her for the world. Maybe a million bucks and a Snickers but not the world.

Epilogue

Nia

X avier had been quiet all morning as we prepared for visitors today. After all of the drama came out with our parents, he had been so intense, so deep in thought. Hopefully, he was able to let his hair down and relax with my family and a few of his friends. I walked into the kitchen where he was prepping the meat to put on the grill, and I handed him his favorite beer.

"Hey, babe, my dad just got here if you want to hang with him. I know all of these women here are going to run you crazy soon."

"Thank God! Somebody else to help me deal with the random "ayes" and twerking you and your sisters like to do."

He chuckled, grabbing the beer from me. He kissed my lips as he headed to the backyard.

The weather was perfect as the sun dipped below the horizon, leaving streaks of purple and orange like soft kisses across the sky. Daddy was huddled in the corner with Xavier and his friends drinking beer and yapping about football. I was glad I hung those patio lights from the trees because it set the vibe with the music flowing. This R&B playlist was hitting, when My Other Gun by Ne-Yo came on, Xavier surprisingly left the guys to get me to dance with him. He knew that Ne-Yo was my favorite artist, so we couldn't miss this. As one song ended, another fave began. Me and You by Tony! Toni! Tone! started playing, and X wrapped me in his arms. We swayed to the beat until he dropped to one knee.

The music played in the background while Xavier gently took my hand, his voice bold and steady as the string lights illuminated behind us.

"Nia, from the moment we met, I was captivated by your beauty. But it was your loyalty, your boldness, and that brilliant, bossy heart of yours that truly claimed me. There is a wildness in you—something untamed—that my soul longs for. I don't want to do life a day without you. Will you marry me?"

As he stood and placed the three-carat, two toned, Art Deco, princess cut, diamond ring on my finger, his lips embraced me in a slow passionate kiss that went on forever. I whispered against his lips as everyone around us went crazy. "Yes, forever yes!"

THANK YOU FOR READING!

*Y*ou've stepped into the shadows... and survived the heat.

I'm so grateful you took a chance on my debut paranormal romance. Whether you're here for the forbidden love, the panther shifters, or the thrill of a secret hunt—thank you for spending time in my world.

Let's Stay Connected

Join my reader list to:

- Get exclusive content (only for subscribers)

- Access future giveaways, book updates, and early cover reveals

- Receive a free bonus scene or epilogue not found in the book

Step into the shadows—> authorstevieo.com

Loved the story? Help me grow!

If you enjoyed the book, a quick review goes a long way in helping other readers find it. Leave a review on:

- **Amazon**

- **Goodreads**

Every word you share supports an indie author chasing a dream in the dark.

What's Next?

- This was only the beginning. Keep an eye out for: Expanding lore of Blackwater Bay

- More heat. More heart. More Hunt.

—

With gratitude and shadow-kissed affection,

Stevie O.

|TikTok:@stevieoauthor | Instagram: AuthorStevie_O | FaceBook: Author Stevie O.

A few excerpts from 5 STAR reviews on Amazon for
ELOHIM—Masters & Minions
Book Two of Winston Trilogy

...a great spin and twist of romance, suspense, depth, conspiracy. It will keep you on your toes and have you turning the pages wanting more of this escape from life, while offering superb mental stimulation. I recommend you get started on this trilogy, you will not be disappointed! Exceptional!

Mary Leckie (Ruskin FL, USA)

The story explores the ramifications of the advancement of genetics and nanotechnology... Dr. Peter Thornton's exploration of humanness deepens as the world vies for power. Mystery and romance punctuate this adventurous, philosophical story, leaving the reader with a deep sense of intellectual stimulation and emotional completeness. Recommended!

J. Linson (USA)

...richly textured page-turner... this book covers quantum physics, spirituality, genetics and androids, with a sprinkling of romance, intrigue, mystery and adventure... Completely engrossing and highly entertaining, this book has my unreserved recommendation.

Monica LaSarre, Author (Colorado, USA)

Once again, the depth of the knowledge that is common in this author's books never fails to amaze me. As with the first book, don't start reading this until you have time to thoroughly digest it, this book needs to be read and savored word by word. I highly recommend.

M. Brown (USA) (TOP 500 REVIEWER)

Stan I.S. Law... paints with intense detail and a wide pallet of colors in this intelligent story full of many moving parts. The science is illuminating, the philosophy intriguing and the human element brilliant. Winston is an amazing character that I think everyone should know. I highly recommend it!

Amy Taylor (USA)

By the same author

ALEC (Alexander Trilogy, Book I)
ALEXANDER (Alexander Trilogy, Book II)
SACHA—The Way Back (Alexander Trilogy, Book III)
YESHUA—Personal Memoir of the Missing Years of Jesus
PETER AND PAUL (An intuitive sequel to Yeshûa)
ONE JUST MAN (Winston Trilogy Book I)
WINSTON'S KINGDOM (Winston Trilogy Book III)
THE AVATAR SYNDROME (Prequel to Headless World)
HEADLESS WORLD—The Vatican Incident
(Sequel to *The Avatar Syndrome*)
MARVIN CLARK–In Search of Freedom
THE GATE—Things My Mother Told Me
NOW—Being and Becoming
GIFT OF GAMMAN
THE PRINCESS
ENIGMA of the Second Coming
WALL—Love, Sex, and Immortality (Aquarius Trilogy Book I)
PLUTO EFFECT [Aquarius Trilogy Book II]
OLYMPUS—Of Gods and Men [Aquarius Trilogy Book III]

Short stories

THE JEWEL & OTHER STORIES
CATS AND DOGS
Sci-Fi Series 1
Sci-Fi Series 2

Non-fiction Books by Stanislaw Kapuscinski

VISUALIZATION—Creating Your Own Universe
KEY TO IMMORTALITY
[Commentary on the Gospel of Thomas]
BEYOND RELIGION: Volumes I, II and III
[Collections of essays on perception of Reality]
DICTIONARY OF BIBLICAL SYMBOLISM
DELUSIONS—Pragmatic Realism

Poetry in Polish
[with illustrations by Bozena Happach]
KILKA SŁÓW I TROCHĘ GLINY
WIĘCEJ SŁÓW I WIĘCEJ GLINY

INHOUSEPRESS, MONTREAL, CANADA
http://inhousepress.ca